N GRAY

Devil Mountain

N. GRAY

Devil
Mountain

VIRAGO
BOOKS

By N Gray

The Dana Mulder Suspense Thriller Series
Deadly Pattern
Devil Mountain
Chasing Evil
Nightcrawler

Vinci Books

vinci-books.com

Published by Vinci Books Ltd in 2025

1

The publisher and the author have made every effort to obtain permissions
for any third party material used in this book and to comply with copyright
law. Any queries in this respect should be brought to the attention of the
publisher and any omissions will be corrected in future editions.
A CIP catalogue record for this book is available from the British Library.
Paperback ISBN: 9781036701765

Chapter One

LIFTING my camera to my face, I watched my target walk into Tiffany's; my finger eased down on the button and took the shot. A few minutes later, he exited with a pretty pink bag in hand. I snapped another picture. I set my camera on the seat beside me, but, before I could dial my client's number, my phone rang with a familiar name on the screen.

"Hello, Dr. Adams," I said.

"Let me guess. You've forgotten about our appointment today."

I cringed in my car seat; to be honest, I had forgotten. I was so busy following my client's ex-husband to Madison, I'd forgotten all about my appointment with my therapist. "Yes," I whispered sheepishly as I watched the ex cross the road and climb into his car.

Dr. Adams sighed so loud I could hear it as if he was sitting beside me; he wasn't happy. "Okay, I can fit you in at the end of the week. Does that sound good?" he asked carefully. He was very accommodating; I'd forgotten my appointment once before, and he had squeezed me in. Previously, I'd asked to move sessions, and he always made a plan for me. I supposed once he knew what I'd been through, he really wanted to help me in any way he could.

"Friday?"

"Yep, say four o'clock?"

As much as I didn't feel like it, I knew I had to go. Dr. Adams was a great listener and made me feel comfortable enough that I would open up and tell him what was on my mind. It didn't hurt he was pleasant to look at—dark hair styled right, bright green eyes, and wore glasses when he took notes. He was professional and put me at ease whenever I felt like I was about to spiral out of control. The previous session, I'd left in tears; it wasn't anything he'd said but what I was going through. The nightmares of Pig-head were still haunting me, and every time I spoke with Johnny, it seemed to bring everything to the surface—again.

"Yeah, four o'clock is fine."

"Is everything okay?"

"All good. Thanks for calling. I have to go, see you Friday." I killed the call before he could respond and quickly dialed my client's number before Dr. Adams could phone back.

"Please tell me you have something!" Maddy cried into my ear, the stress of everything evident in her tone.

I stifled a joyous laugh, trying to put myself into a good mood after my call with Dr. Adams but failed miserably, and Maddy shrieked. "I got him, Maddy," I finally said, not wanting to keep her anxious.

Maddy shrieked again.

Her ex had been telling the judge he was bankrupt and unable to pay my client child support. She suspected he had hidden money during the divorce, and he had a new girl-friend by the time the proceedings started, which made her more suspicious. Now with him going into the jewelry story, I suspected the new girlfriend was about to be his new fiancée.

"What did you get?"

"Uhm, he was walking out of a jewelry store." I winced as I said the words. I knew Maddy still loved her ex and was in denial after the divorce. If she knew he wanted to marry another—if what I assumed was correct—I wasn't sure how she would handle it: confront and attack him or continue with the legal route. "Are you sure you want the details?"

"He's going to marry her, isn't he?" She sighed audibly.

"I don't know—"

"Okay, it's okay. It's really okay. Send it to my lawyer and tell him to let me know what the judge says."

I exhaled. That was the best thing she could do for her family. "No problem, Maddy. You just take care of your beautiful girls. Let your lawyer handle the rest."

"I know you're right. And, Dana …?"

"Yeah?"

"Thanks for helping me."

"It's a pleasure."

"You doing this for me, and for free, has helped us. When the jackass starts paying, I will take you out for a lunch somewhere."

"That's perfect. You take care now."

As I ended the call, it rang again. It was Johnny—my direct report when I had worked as an analyst for the FBI. We had kept in touch all these years and spoke at least once a month to catch up. I would even ask him for guidance on cases I was working, and he always obliged to help. It was strange he was calling again, since we had already spoken last week. For him to call again, had to be urgent.

"Hey—"

"Dana! I need your help."

"What's wrong?"

"It's not me. It's my sister."

Chapter Two

I WAS on the road again, but, instead of heading home toward Chicago, I was driving farther in the opposite direction toward Wisconsin. Something had happened at Devil Mountain, and Johnny needed me to go there. He had called and asked for a favor. His sister and her two daughters were camping, and, when his mom couldn't get hold of her, they called the park ranger at Devil Mountain to search for them. They found their camp site, but they weren't there. Search and rescue had been called, along with cadaver dogs. His parents were not in a position to travel immediately, and since the violent attack by Pig-head and his vigilante killers, Johnny had suffered a major spinal cord injury that could not be repaired and was left wheelchair bound with a machine helping him breathe. Unfortunately, it made things difficult for him to get around and couldn't do certain things himself. He and his parents would fly from Florida as soon as they could, but, in the meantime, he had asked that I represent him until they got here.

Although Johnny had plenty of friends on the various

police forces and in the FBI, I didn't have any of the red tape that came with it. He needed my help on this case— and now—and I would be there for him.

I drove slowly through the winding roads that would lead me to the ranger's cabin at the foot of Devil Mountain, which bordered between Wisconsin and Illinois. On any other day, the scenic drive would be wonderful—the tall trees on either side, the fresh air, and wild animals made for a great nature escape. Instead, the drive filled me with dread not knowing what I was about to walk into— would Olivia and the girls be found, and would they be alive?

Devil's Mountain during the winter months would be full of snow, ski slopes, and cabins full of people holding mugs with marshmallows and hot cocoa. While during the summer months, there were hiking trails, beautiful scenery, and spectacular waterfalls. Currently, the days were sunny and the evenings cooler as we headed into autumn.

Following the GPS directions, I meandered up a narrow road until I came upon a row of cop cars. I slowly drove past the cars until a man in a dark uniform flagged me down.

"Sorry, ma'am, but the hiking trail is closed for today. You can come back next week."

"I'm not here to hike. The brother of the missing woman called me in."

"What's your name?"

"Dana Mulder."

The cop turned away from me and whispered into his radio. When he was done, he turned back to me. "You still can't be here." He sounded unhappy with each word he spat.

I felt the lines between my eyes deepen. Glancing at the

officer's name badge, I grabbed my phone and punched Johnny's number.

"Have you spoken with Brent yet?" Johnny asked hoarsely. The sound of his monitors flared to life as his excitement grew.

"Not yet. Officer Bradley stopped me from going anywhere. Are you sure I'm allowed to be here?" I asked loud enough for the officer to hear.

Officer Bradley grunted in what I could only assume was dissatisfaction of the use of his name.

"Tell Officer Bradley that Detective Fletcher arranged for you to be there. I will hang on while you tell him."

"Officer Bradley," I said *officer* with an edge of sarcasm, "Detective Fletcher is expecting me. Please can you tell whoever it is you are speaking with on your little radio that I'm allowed to be here?"

Officer Bradley's jaw clenched, and his mouth flattened into a straight line. I caught some tightening around his blue eyes as he narrowed them at me.

I offered him my best blank face.

He turned and whispered into his radio. Whatever was said to him made his face redden. His nostrils flared when he turned to me. He bent down and rested his elbows on my window.

I leaned backward so my face wasn't right in front of his.

"Kindly turn around and park behind the other cruisers. Then you can walk back up here," he said in a low baritone.

"Thank you." I offered him my friendliest smile. I wasn't sure why I had received a hostile reception, but it came with the job sometimes. I was a female private investigator, and sometimes men in uniform didn't appreciate it. I pulled away with him still hanging on my window, but the moment the car moved, he stood and stepped backward. I could feel his glare at the back of my head as I turned my vehicle around.

Only once I had parked and started the walk up did I notice the scenery. James and I should definitely hike here one weekend. Devil Mountain was part of a trust and on private property. The owners opened the trail and accommodation facilities the first week of every month. They charged a hefty fee, but they had to in order to pay a full-time ranger.

Officer Bradley was nowhere to be seen when I reached the ranger cabin; instead, a lanky man with short red hair, green eyes, and a friendly smile greeted me.

"Dana," he said with an outstretched hand. "I'm Detective Fletcher. Please call me Stephen."

When Johnny had first called, he had informed me he and Detective Fletcher had trained together many moons ago and kept in contact. He was also the lead detective on his sister's case. I guessed Johnny did pull a string to get him on board and for me to tag along without any questions asked. Although it might answer the question why Officer Bradley was hostile toward me. Johnny must've phoned him after my little run in with Officer Bradley. I shook his warm hand.

"It's a pleasure to meet you. Sorry it's under these circumstances though."

"What has Johnny told you?" His response was curt and to the point but said with a pleasant enough smile and kind eyes.

"Not much, that his sister and her two daughters are missing after they went camping." I shrugged and followed him toward the cabin.

We entered the cabin, and Stephen handed me a bottle of water and a flashlight. "My team is currently processing the scene. When we suspected they were missing and couldn't get hold of Brent, Olivia's husband, I phoned Johnny." He slung his backpack over his shoulder. "After a thorough search of the camp site, we found her."

"Is she okay?" I scanned the cabin. "Where is she?"

Stephen's expression changed to one that people reserved for funerals or delivering bad news, and my heart sank to my toes. The news would devastate Johnny and his parents.

"And the girls?" I swallowed hard and opened the bottle of water for a drink.

"They're still missing."

"Oh no, and you haven't gotten hold of Brent yet?" I'd met Brent once when I visited Johnny after the attack. He had been busy on a conference call and only waved at me in greeting. Olivia had been welcoming and her two girls precious; one was nine and the other thirteen. I'd visited Johnny again after that, and the three girls were there as well—they were a lovely family.

"No." He shook his head. "We keep getting his voice-mail." He reached for the door and opened it. "Do you hike often?"

"Yes, quite regularly actually. My backpack is in the trunk."

"Great. The more eyes we have on this the better."

Stephen and I exited the cabin toward my car. James and I always kept our backpacks in the trunk of our cars just in case we wanted to go for an afternoon hike after work. But, when I opened my trunk, I realized I had left my boots at home. My sneakers would have to do.

Chapter Three

STEPHEN HAD MENTIONED their camp site was an hour and a half hike up the mountain. Due to the tall trees and dense vegetation, we had to walk and could not use the helicopter. The winding path had taken us toward a stream deeper alongside the mountain with hundreds of trees and green vegetation. It was cooler in the shade as we neared the stream, and the sounds of water falling over rocks was therapeutic. Old trees had fallen to the ground and had started to turn a dull green-gray color.

Stephen walked ahead while I glanced upstream where the trees were denser, and thick branches covered in leaves obscured something. Stephen wasn't walking too fast, so I could catch up to him, but I wanted to know what it was. The closer I got, the more I realized someone was in the bushes. Shadows from the trees left me in a blanket of darkness, and I turned back to see where Stephen was; his back was to me as he walked farther away.

"Hello?" I called out.

They didn't move. It looked like they had their back to me, sitting in a wall of leaves.

Stephen had heard me yell and turned back as I approached the person, but they were motionless.

Walking around it, I gasped and stepped backward.

"Hey, you found him." Stephen joined me; his smile reached his eyes. "Do you know how long I've been looking for this guy?"

"What is it?"

"It's part of the trail, something fun for hikers to look out for." He sounded pleased. "After all the years I've come out here with my boy, we had never seen him. You come here and find him on your first hike." He playfully slapped my shoulder.

I reached to touch its face. "Someone carved a man out of wood and left him here for people to find?" The wood carving was of a man sitting meditation style with his hand to his face and a finger to his mouth—*remain silent.* Whoever had produced this piece of art had taken pride in their job; the detail was exquisite on the face, making it lifelike.

"Yeah, we think it's the same person leaving the dolls."

My arms pebbled. "There's dolls as well?"

"You'll see them up ahead." He glanced at the high tree branches.

A shudder ran through me. "I won't lie to you, but this is a strange hiking trail."

"It's Devil Mountain, Dana. It's freaky, but at least it's pretty."

"Yeah, they hid him well," I said as I stared at the carving. We turned to get back on the trail. "Is this the only one, or are there more of him? That way I know not to shoot the person if he was carved with his arm pointed at me." I laughed, but it sounded hollow.

Stephen chuckled. "Apparently, there are six of them, but I have no idea where the others are."

"Six?"

"If you find another one, your next drink is on me," he said jokingly, but then his demeanor shifted to sullen.

We were heading toward a crime scene, our friends' sister's. I felt guilty for smiling and suspected so did Stephen. Birds flew above our heads, and I flinched at the sudden noise. They perched atop branches, whistling at neighbors. The trees were alive with crawling insects, and luckily, there were no snakes from what I could see.

I dusted sand and ants off the side of my pants, removed my backpack from my shoulder and had a drink of water. My feet already ached in my sneakers, but it was nothing compared to what Johnny and his family would be going through shortly. I was not looking forward to that phone call, but, before I did that, I wanted to see the scene for myself so I could answer any of Johnny's questions.

Once my backpack was on my shoulder, I beheld the scenery again as we hiked. I stopped dead when a head caught my eye. At first, I thought it was a child stuck high on a tree, dangling from a branch, but it was only a doll head with one eyelid open and the other stuck midway, with stains smeared all over its face. I shuddered at the sight.

Stephen chuckled when he turned to see why I wasn't behind him. "Yeah, you've found the first of many. They're all over this place. Whoever did it placed them so high nobody has the energy to take them down. Don't let them spook you."

"I'm not spooked. It just caught me off guard for a second. I'd never seen such a thing while hiking before." The lines between my brow deepened.

"People do strange things when in nature."

"I'll bet."

As we continued, I kept looking up in case there were more. I'd counted seven doll heads in various state of deterioration. Some heads were chopped in half, others at the neck; the elements had dirtied and soiled them all. And none of the eyes worked. I felt imaginary insects climb up my arms.

To break the silence, Stephen asked me questions. "Do you have a place to stay, or are you driving back to Chicago tonight?"

"Johnny has arranged a hotel for me."

Stephen didn't respond, and the silence felt awkward, so I continued the exchange. "Johnny tells me you guys trained together." I jumped across a stream and saw another doll swinging upside down, its white plastic hair stained with dirt and missing both eyes.

"Yeah, I applied at the FBI first, and that's when I met him. Unfortunately, I didn't make it and went into law enforcement instead. And we've stayed in touch since. It was terrible what happened to him—and you, of course."

"Johnny got most of the beating, and we lost three other agents that day. I was lucky they left me alone."

"But that man is still after you, isn't he?"

It had been four months since the shootout when James and I had hiked. James had been hit in the shoulder, and we suspected I had hit Pig-head, and he too was recovering, because I hadn't heard from him since. Forensics had collected blood at the crime scene, and we had assumed it was DNA, and Donnie had it processed. He had gotten positive hits on CODIS for samples found at four unrelated crimes, but there had been no positive match to the samples —until now. We could tie Pig-head to these crimes, but we didn't know who he was. Even though Pig-head wasn't currently after me, it didn't mean I could stop looking over my shoulder.

"Yeah, he is still around somewhere," I said sounding deflated.

"And your boyfriend doesn't mind you going off on your own?"

"How do you know who my boyfriend is?"

"Detective James Michaels, isn't it?"

"Ye-es." I narrowed my eyes at Stephen.

"Johnny and I speak regularly."

What I didn't tell Stephen was Johnny and I had discussed my one and only case with the FBI. That was my reason at first for keeping in contact with Johnny; I wanted to find out what the FBI was doing about Pig-head and his vigilante killers. Johnny had told me they were still under investigation, but, after our attack, they had gone underground. The FBI had no idea who they were or what had happened to them. And there were no more murders attributed to the killers; it was as if they too had disappeared following the attack. The only reason I knew Pig-head was still around was because of the gifts he'd sent and the attack on James and I. Johnny had said that when the FBI heard about that, they started the investigation again with a new task team, but he wasn't sure whether they would speak with me about what had happened, and I hadn't heard from them either, so I continued as if they weren't around. If anything was to be done about Pig-head, it would be done by me; I wouldn't wait for the FBI's assistance, but that didn't mean I didn't want to know what they had.

"So do we, but I'd never heard of you until today."

"My life is pretty boring, so there wouldn't have been

anything for Johnny to tell you. My divorce is a common occurrence and nothing to write home about."

"I'm sorry."

"It's fine, one of those things. Well?"

"Well, what?"

"What does James think about you doing things on your own?"

"Oh, that. Well, at first, we were worried that Pig-head would come after me again. But after James was hit, we took precautions. But we haven't heard from Pig-head since then." I heard people speaking up ahead; we were nearing the crime scene. "Do you know James?" Illinois and Wisconsin were big, but I didn't know if all the cops knew each other from different jurisdictions.

"We all heard what had happened, but I knew more than most because of what Johnny had told me. But I don't know James personally."

Chapter Four

YELLOW TAPE STOPPED me from entering the crime scene.

"Wait here," Stephen said, lifted the tape and went under. "I'm going to see how far they are but come around this side. There's a better view for you from over there." He waved me to the right, and I followed, going around the scene.

A blue dome tent stood to one side next to a dead fire, and paper plates were scattered on top of the wooden table. The area was large enough for at least ten tents where campers could stay the night, sit at tables and eat while enjoying festive fires and nature around them. Trees littered the campsite, and a small ablution block sat in the middle split for male and female where campers could shower. The ground had litter but not much. Clothing was scattered outside the tent, with a backpack ripped to shreds. I followed the yellow tape until I stood to one side near the dome tent and could see the technicians work at collecting evidence. Off to one side and down the mountain, pale skin was hidden under dense vegetation. The coroner crouched near her body and spoke with Stephen who nodded in response.

No bears were in the area to leave a mess, therefore whoever was here didn't do a great job at masking their actions. I held onto the yellow crime scene tape to ensure I didn't snap it as I leaned over to get a better look. I could see inside the dome tent—three thin mattresses beside each other with three sleeping bags. There were socks, shoes, and a jersey but only the one backpack. Two backpacks were missing, if Olivia's two daughters were with her. Had someone taken them? Had they witnessed their mom's murder? Did they run away, or did the person who killed Olivia take them with?

Something caught my eye. I glanced up to see Stephen waving again and calling me over. I followed the yellow line until I was close enough to the body without crossing the threshold.

A knot formed in the pit of my stomach when I saw her dark hair among the dead leaves. The last time I'd seen her, she was laughing and playing catch with their dog while Ava and Charlotte tried to hold onto the dog—bouts of laughter and happy tears filled the afternoon sunset. Her emerald-colored eyes held so much love for her family and welcomed me as if we were longtime friends. A pang of pain hit my chest, and I didn't want to make the phone call to Johnny, even though I had to. It had to be me.

Olivia's pale skin held a grey and purple-blue tint, and I was grateful she faced the other direction and I couldn't see her face or soulless eyes. All I saw was her side and black hair. Her shirt was torn near her shoulder but was still clothed. Her attacker hadn't strangled her, and I couldn't see any blunt force trauma to her head.

"She was shot in the face," Stephen said, pulling me from my thoughts.

"There was a struggle." I pointed to her clothing that was pulled off her shoulder.

"Yep. Shot point blank." He pointed to his eye for further visual explanation. "No exit wound so the bullet is still in her head. She died instantly and fell where she was standing."

A shudder ran through me as I hoped she hadn't felt anything. I didn't see any drag marks near her resting place; she was most likely having an argument with her attacker under the trees, then fell soon after the gun went off. I glanced at the tent, which was a distance away. If the girls were still in the tent, perhaps they saw what had happened. I silently hoped they could tell us who it was but, at the same time, not—no child should witness their parents' murder.

"They could've seen what happened." I pointed to the tent. "She sees someone she knows. Comes out here under the trees to speak with them. Maybe they argue, the girls see what's happening, and, before she's killed, she tells the girls to hide." I glanced behind me at the dense forest and steep cliff to one side. "Do you have anyone searching for them?"

"Yep, and we've called in cadaver dogs," he said with gloom etched on his face. "We should expect them to be here soon." He glanced at his cellphone. "It gets cold here at night, and, if the girls are out there and are lost, they could freeze. Or they may be hurt. They've already been outside for one evening, and I really don't want them out here for another night."

"Were they looking for something?" I pointed to the ripped backpack and strewn clothing.

"Maybe, or the kids were in a hurry to get away. It'll

take a while to process everything, but we will find out who was here. If it's the only case I work on, I will find out who did this." His voice broke near the end, and he looked away.

"Do you mind if I walk around the area?"

"Be my guest, but I would advise not to venture out too far. It'll be dark soon, and I don't think you want to be lost out here."

"I'll be fine. Can I have your number in case I find something?"

He said his number, and I entered it into my phone and gave him a missed call so he could save my number.

Chapter Five

FOUR HIKING trails led from the campsite. I traversed the path I would use if I saw my mom gunned down and needed to hide in a hurry. When I stood behind the dome tent, I saw a path on the right that seemed to dip down the mountain. I pulled the map from my backpack to see where I was heading. One could take different types of hiking trails, and, from what I could see, this one was longer and one of the more difficult ones, with rocks a hiker would have to climb over.

Stephen had said a search party was assigned to each of the trails. If I was trying to get away from someone, I wouldn't stay on the path. I would want to hide deeper inside the vegetation so nobody could see me.

This trail had a tree canopy to shelter hikers from the scorching sun. The deeper I walked, the eager the shadows crept closer. I strolled, watching the ground for any sign the girls may have been here, but it was impossible to tell if what I saw were footprints or not. The hairs on my arms pebbled, and I glanced up to see another doll; a shudder ran through me. I hated dolls—especially these ones. I surveyed the area for any hiding places.

My cellphone rang—James. I'd been so busy I'd forgotten to let him know where I was.

"Hey, babe, where are you?" he asked.

"I'm past Madison."

"What in god's name are you doing out there? I thought you were in Rockford."

"I was in Rockford, but then something happened—"

"Are you okay? Should I call somebody to come get you?"

"No, I'm fine. Johnny asked for my help. At first, his sister was reported missing, but they found her body. But her two daughters are still missing, and I'm helping them look for them."

"Oh, no." A few seconds of silence stretched between us. He was thinking; I could actually hear the cogs of his mind move. We had been a couple for about four months and had already learned each other's quirks and mannerisms. When James was this quiet, he was worried. "When are you coming back?" he finally asked.

After Pig-head's attacks, we had spent every single night together, either at his house or at mine. I had moved into a new house which came with an upgrade in security features and a twenty-four-hour guard. And, as much as I loved my independence, I loved having James around more and more with each passing day.

"I'm not sure, a couple of days maybe. I wanted to ask you. I know it's almost a three-hour drive to get here, but would you be willing to come this way and stay with me in the hotel Johnny is paying for? Order some takeout and watch something, or do other things?" I smiled and hoped he could hear the hint in my voice.

I really wanted him to come through and spend the night with me. It would be nice to see him when I was done here. Seeing the dolls and strange carvings had creeped me out, but seeing Olivia like that was worse. Every time I witnessed something evil where someone was hurting others out of spite, jealousy, or just for fun, the more I appreciated what was in front of me. I may be the object of some sicko's affection, but I was grateful to have James in my life, and so far things were great—not perfect, because nothing was ever perfect—and we seemed to be a wonderful fit for each other. And we weren't young, where we played games with each other for attention; we said what was on our minds, and, if we wanted to stay together, then that's what we did.

"Do you need me to bring you an overnight bag?" He chuckled lightly.

"Yes, please, if you don't mind."

"Not at all, I would love to see you. Besides, I need my back rub."

James was still recovering from the day we were attacked while hiking—one of the worst days of my life. After the helicopter had taken him away, Donnie and I had first helped to collect the evidence Pig-head had left behind. When we finally had arrived at the hospital, the staff had told us that James was out of recovery and in ICU. My feelings for James had developed rather quickly, and I hadn't realized it until Donnie and I entered James's room and I saw him lying on the bed helpless, injured, and with tubes everywhere. The sound of that monitor beeping was imprinted in my brain, and I would never forget it. We were his only family, and I had sat by his side until he recovered fully. The bullet had gone through his shoulder, and they had to repair the damage to his scapular. Luckily, there was no nerve damage, and the doctors had made his shoulder whole again with a few pins and plenty of stitches. However, he had lost a lot of blood and needed rest. They had discharged him a week later into my tender loving care. And, since then, his shoulder would freeze in the evenings after a long day at work, and only after a proper rub down of his back would he feel as good as new.

"Yes, you need to take your prescribed medication," I teased. "Doctor's orders."

"You don't want a cranky detective on your hands anyway."

"Oh no, a cranky detective is not welcomed in my home."

"You only want a happy detective?" James asked in a playful, seductive voice.

"Yes, I only want a happy detective."

I heard men's laughter in the background, then James whispered into the mouthpiece, "I've got to go. Send me your hotel details, and I'll see you around nine."

"Okay," I said and laughed. If that was Donnie in the background, poking fun at James, he would not be able to escape it. "I'll let you know if I'm still out here though. We may be here all night."

"Keep me posted."

Chapter Six

I'D JUST PUT my phone away when screams pierced the afternoon air. I ran to the campsite to chaos erupting around us. Stephen and two others ran across the campsite on the other side of the ablution block. We ran in the direction of the cries, crossing through dense vegetation, over rocks, and between trees. Not wanting to be left behind, I pursued after Stephen.

The cries sounded again; whoever it was, they were off the trail, forcing us to climb over a rock and slide down. I followed the others and stumbled over a log, crashing to the ground knees first. My chest ached as I hoped it was the girls but, at the same time, not—they were hurt and crying, and, from the cries, it was only one person. From my view from the grassy floor, others moved through the trees to the rescue up ahead. I stood, dusted my pants and walked to where a crowd had already formed. On the other side of a bush was a hole with everyone standing as far back as they could but still able to see in.

An officer had fallen about ten feet into a hole and was

holding his leg; his shin had broken and pierced his skin. His face was etched in pain with beads of sweat peppering his forehead.

THE SKY HELD streaks of red and orange as darkness bled into dusk. I ate my last snack—a packet of nuts—and sipped my water. I sat on a rock and watched the commotion taking place below.

The tech team were still processing the crime scene, while most of the volunteers and officers were still searching for Ava and Charlotte. I stayed with Stephen and three others with Dennis, the officer who had fallen into the hole. Dennis had thought he saw one of the girls, had walked off the path and had fallen into a pit. The unstable ground beneath him had given way under his weight. As it turned out, what he had seen was a pink blanket, which we suspect belonged to one of the girls. The wind could've brought the blanket this side, or the girls had dropped it as they ran.

Edward, an officer who scaled rocks as a hobby, had gone into the hole with a stretcher to fetch Dennis. With his leg in a tourniquet, they had hoisted Dennis out of the hole while Edward had searched inside. It was just a hole.

The rescue team had retrieved Dennis and carried him to the ambulance waiting for him at the ranger cabin. He would go straight to the OR where they would repair the bone in his leg.

Crouching, I picked up two branches that lay around the hole. Holding the branches, I strode to show Stephen. "The branches were cut." I handed him the branches so he could see. "Someone cut them on purpose, covered the hole and waited for someone to fall in."

Stephen took them from me.

"Do you think someone does this to hunt the animals that roam the mountain?"

"If anyone was hunting, they would've used guns and only in season. But you aren't allowed to hunt here." He surveyed the area with hawk eyes. The pulse in Stephen's neck seemed to bulge as the lines near his eyes tightened. He called one of the officers to him to collect the branches for testing to determine how they were cut.

To me, they all seemed cut with a sharp knife and not hacked or pulled from the trees. A sinking feeling engulfed me; all this had happened, and we were no close to finding the girls. There wasn't even a sign they had been here—only the possibility that someone had taken them was much higher.

"Has anyone gotten hold of Brent yet?"

"No," Stephen answered as he scouted the area. "The cadaver dogs are on their way up. We should head to the campsite to welcome their handler."

The tone from my cellphone broke my concentration. I showed Stephen my screen; it was Johnny. "What do I tell him?"

"Everything."

I exhaled deeply. "Hey."

"I can't get through to Stephen's cell. Can you please tell me what's happening?" Johnny sounded as tired as I felt, and I didn't know an easy way to tell him. I just had to get it out.

"Johnny, I need to tell you something ..." I relayed the events of finding his sister but that the girls were still missing; and we wouldn't stop searching until we found them.

"Oh gods, I don't know what to tell our parents. This might kill them."

"I'm sorry, Johnny. I really am. They haven't been able to reach Brent. Do you have another number we can use?"

"He doesn't know?"

"No. They can't get hold of him."

"I only have his cell. Wait, he has a personal assistant." He gave me her number, and I read it out for Stephen.

"Thanks. Take care of yourself, and I will call the moment we have something." I ended the call and dialed Marc's number.

I'd been sending him text messages, giving him updates about the two cases, but hadn't actually spoken to him since yesterday. I'd sent him the photos of my client's ex-husband entering the jewelry store and exiting with a bag along with a receipt I'd picked up after he dropped it near a bank; it showed a very healthy bank balance. With some reverse clarification, we discovered it was his bank account and not his new girlfriend's. He hadn't been paying alimony for over a year, claiming bankruptcy, and had hid his other bank account. With the proof he was in good standing, Marc knew a judge and had called in a favor to hear the case this afternoon. Once presented with the evidence, the judge had called an urgent meeting. Marc informed me the judge took fifteen minutes to decide, and, if the ex didn't pay by the end of the week, he would issue an arrest warrant.

"Thanks. That was really fast."

"All in a day's work. Besides, the judge is a fishing buddy."

I explained where I was and what had happened and that we were still looking for the girls.

"Do you need Nigel to join you?"

Marc and Nigel kept me in the dark when it came to what Nigel could or couldn't do, and what Marc was saying was that he could assist. There was no way I would pass up on that offer. Something about this case made my skin crawl as much as Pig-head did. And we needed to confirm whether the person leaving traps was doing so for hunting animals and not hikers.

"Is Nigel some sort of tracker?" I asked, trying to get more insight into his day job.

"Something like that." Marc offered, but that was all. "Okay, Nigel is near the area and can be there shortly to help with the search."

"Thanks," I said and ended the call.

I watched Stephen and some other officers finish what they were doing and collect the rope from the hole and place a makeshift barrier around it. Even though the hiking trails were closed to the public, anyone could fall inside it again when it was dark—at least with the bright tape, they could be warned.

"Night is falling," Stephen said when he approached. "It looks like we'll be here all night, but, if you prefer to come back tomorrow morning, you are welcome to. But, if you are staying, I hope you brought something warm. It can get pretty cool out here."

"I'll stay, thanks. And I brought something." I took that as a cue to remove my jacket from my backpack.

The gold and sharp pinks highlighted the sky as the sun kissed us goodnight. I sent James a text, letting him know I would be here for a few more hours.

Chapter Seven

WHILE STEPHEN COORDINATED the scene with his partner's help, I strolled the trail to a spot where the trees were denser, shadows played on the dark green leaves, and wild bushes filled the area. Leaves rustled beside me, and I froze. My pulse thundered in my ears, taking me back to my hike with James when we were ambushed. I'd consulted with Dr. Adams on a monthly basis after that, and I'd managed to sleep longer than four hours a night this last month and without breaking into a sweat each time. As I turned to see what was behind me, a squirrel ran up a tree off to the left. I swallowed my fear and wiped my damp hands on my pants.

I'd walked to a spot where I had view of the hole Dennis had fallen into and of the cops at the crime scene on the campsite, the standard yellow tape surrounding the spots visible through the green. I took a wide girth around both areas and descended the mountain but off the path. If the girls had run away and wanted to hide, perhaps they were here somewhere. Also, I hoped they hadn't fallen into another hole, if a hunter was out here setting traps.

I saw more doll heads hanging by their necks on high tree branches and blocked them out. I came across fallen trees and disturbed bushes near a stream, and the sound was a gentle lullaby as the water moved over rocks. Broken tree branches lay inside mud, stones overturned, and young trees leaned to the same side. The area must've had rain which flooded the area and brought debris with it. Now that everything was normal again, the devastation remained.

Glancing around, I'd spotted something under the fallen trees that didn't sit right with nature and approached it with caution. I crouched to grab a stick and poked it. I lifted the material to reveal jeans. What I wasn't expecting was a femur bone rising with it, unravelling and falling to the ground. I jumped backward to avoid it hitting my shoes and yelled for Stephen.

———

STEPHEN CURSED under his breath after I showed him my discovery. "Do you always have the habit of finding bodies?" he asked rhetorically. "At least it's not the girls. I wonder who the poor chap was." He leaned over the fallen tree and opened the blue shirt that clung to the skeletal remains.

In the shallow grave was a weathered shoe that had most likely come off the victim when he either fell or was placed there. His corpse had decomposed into the soil or had been nibbled on by animals and insects. His jeans were still intact, except the bottoms were frayed from the usual wear and tear from standing on them. The area had experienced a few downpours, and it was possible the sand had washed away from the shallow grave, exposing the remains to the elements until I came across it.

Stephen inspected the surrounding area. "Seems to be male, but once Clive does his magic, we will know who he was, how he died, and time of death. And, with any luck, maybe who the killer was."

Clive clucked his tongue. "You wish, Detective." He too peered over the fallen tree. "I can promise I'll try my best. It's been out here for ages, so who knows what we will find? You, on the other hand, will have to do all the heavy lifting. Judging by our skeleton's choice of fashion, he's been out here at least ten years."

Stephen sighed.

Clive stood with a body bag while his assistants scooped tons of sand for processing along with anything near the remains for sorting and testing.

Stephen would be busy all evening with the three crime scenes, and we were nowhere near finding the girls. "Are you sure you want to hang out here? It's getting late, and this might take all night." He sighed as he glanced around.

"I'm staying," I confirmed.

"Thanks. The cadaver dogs should be here shortly." He checked his watch. "Let's walk to the campsite."

The night swarmed around us as we reached the campsite. I texted James to give him the name of the hotel I was at and that the hotel knew I would check in later and was expecting him. I wanted to see him even if it was only for a short while. I knew he had work tomorrow, and I would most likely still be on this case for Johnny. If we had a chance to see one another, I wanted it.

Stephen approached the dog handler who was speaking with his partner, Justin Fleming. Justin was soft around the edges and looked like someone who gave cuddly hugs. His head was shaved and shone under the lamps surrounding the campsite, and he tended to rub his goatee when asked his opinion on things. Stephen had mentioned him to me during our hike and called me over to introduce us now that things had calmed down.

Justin gazed over me like the wind and didn't give me a second glance. He grunted in greeting without shaking my hand; instead, he turned to speak with the dog handler so they could find the girls. I didn't mind, just as long as we found the girls.

"Sorry, he doesn't like outsiders working with us," Stephen said when Justin was out of earshot. "Our captain did a-okay you being here, and it isn't as if you're the one collecting evidence, so I don't know what's eating him."

"Don't worry about it. I think we all want to find the girls and get out of here."

"Yeah, or he's just jealous you found the skeleton. Which means he has to write the report." He chuckled. "Come, the dogs are about to head out."

I watched the handler open a bag that's believed to belong to one of the girls.

His bloodhound and beagle barked continuously and pulled on their leashes. He eventually released them.

Justin ran behind in a cross between a gallop and a strange limp.

Stephen took off, and I followed. The dogs' bark surrounded the forest as we ran, making my arms pebble. Birds flew overhead, and the only thing I heard was my heart beating.

Chapter Eight

MY LUNGS BURNED as we ran on the trail I had originally thought the girls might have taken. The bloodhound veered off the path, with the beagle close behind it; they ran through thick vegetation, under and over dead trees. They'd picked up the girl's scent, and I prayed we would find them soon—and alive.

Justin lagged behind us, out of breath, with Stephen and I right behind the handler.

His dogs stopped near a rocky area and barked like crazy at something behind it. As we neared, shrill cries echoed around us. The handler leashed his two dogs, gave them water in a portable bowl and rubbed their heads; *good boys*.

Stephen and I followed the cries. Wedged between two rocks, we found the girls in each other's arms. Tears streaked their faces, and wide eyes blinked back at us. Dirt caked their bodies as if they had crawled through mud on their hands and knees. I glanced to the right of the rocks and saw the path they'd used; they came around the rocks, which was steeper than the trail we'd just taken, and had skidded down. Since it had been raining, more mud was this side than on the path. Then they sheltered here, too afraid to come out. They were a distance away from the campsite, therefore I doubted they couldn't hear that we were here. I suspected the dogs barking and pursuing them had caused tension to rise within them again, making them cry.

Their wailing subsided when I pushed Stephen to the side and approached them, like one would a frightened animal. Their whimpers quietened, but they still clung to each other for dear life.

"Are you hurt?" I asked.

They flinched but said nothing. They blinked misty green eyes.

"Do you want some water?"

They flinched again at the sound of my voice but nodded this time.

I pulled an unopened bottle from my backpack, opened it and handed it to them.

The oldest, Charlotte, gave it to her sister Ava first, then she had some. They shared it until it was finished.

Stephen handed me another bottle, which I handed slowly to Charlotte again.

"Can you point to anywhere on your body to let me know if you are hurt?"

Charlotte shook her head while Ava stared at me, through me, and I doubted she saw me.

Three paramedics had been stationed at the campsite for when we found the girls, and, since the ambulance had left with Dennis, Stephen had to call to confirm the ambulance was returning to fetch the girls. One sprinted toward us with two more following, all three armed with first-aid kits and stretchers.

"There are paramedics coming to ensure you are all right. Do you think you can manage them looking you over?" I asked as I stood out of their way.

Charlotte nodded.

"I think they're traumatized," I said to Stephen when I was out of earshot.

The paramedics were gentle with them and patient as they assessed the girls for injury.

"Yeah, I think they saw something. I've notified the hospital. They are ready with doctors and a child psychologist."

"Good. They'll need it." I said and glanced at the sisters. The paramedics had covered them with blankets. "I'm just glad they're okay. Well, they're not okay, but alive. What about Brent?"

"His assistant got hold of him. He was apparently in a meeting last night and again today. He switched his cell-phone to silent before the first meeting started and forgot to switch it back. The assistant had to phone the offices, where he was to reach him. He's on his way here now."

"Where was he?"

"Chicago."

I felt something behind me; that eery feeling when you knew someone was watching. When I turned, I saw Nigel walking up the trail and smiled.

"Hey, cupcake," he said as he approached.

"Hey, Nigel." I introduced him to Stephen and excused myself. "I'd forgotten you were coming. So much has happened since I last spoke with Marc. We might not need your skills after all. We found the girls."

"No worries. I'll be here if you need me all the same," he said as he watched Stephen speak to the medics.

I glanced at Nigel and my brows furrowed; his mousy

hair was brushed and neatly out of his face, but his beard was longer. His smile seemed to brighten his face and brown eyes when he had seen me.

"What's with the beard? You going grizzly on me?"

"I haven't had time to shave."

"Jeez, you've had no time for weeks then. Your face looks better without the facial hair, by the way. Unless your lady-love can't get enough of the fur?"

"Nah, I've just been really busy." His eyes creased at the corners when he glanced at me. "Marc says they haven't gotten hold of the husband yet."

"I was just chatting with Stephen, and they found Brent. He's been in meetings all this time and is on his way."

He tapped his fingers on the side of his leg, a nervous twitch.

"When did you see Marc last? Is he coping in the office without us there?"

"Marc is fine. You don't have to worry about him. What's next?" He surveyed the commotion.

"Actually, I'm exhausted. We found the girls, and they are busy processing the scenes—"

"Scenes? I thought it was just the one. How many are there?"

"Someone fell into a hole that seems to be manmade. It was covered in branches cut from trees. I found skeletal remains, which they had to dig up and process, and then the camp site where they found Olivia." I whispered the last part; I didn't want her kids to hear.

"Trust you to find another dead person." Nigel smirked and elbow bumped me. "Soon nobody will want you on their case."

"It was an accident. I was looking for the girls when I stumbled across the remains."

He arched a bushy eyebrow at me.

"I swear." I stifled a yawn. The time on my cellphone read 8:55 p.m., and I still had to hike to my car. My body ached, and I was hungry for proper food and a glass of wine. I sent James a text to let him know I was leaving and should be at the hotel just after 10 p.m. "Are you staying for the evening, or are you driving back home?"

"As much as I don't like staying in these types of places, I am and staying at the same place as you so we can drive together tomorrow. That should be fun." He wiggled his eyebrows.

"Are you here to keep me safe?"

He snorted back a laugh. "I know you can keep yourself safe, cupcake. But Marc needs me to help you wrap this one up. Your stack of cases is piling up back home, so hurry up already."

With Pig-head nowhere in sight, I suspected it wouldn't last for long and was grateful to have Nigel around—just in case. If Pig-head was keeping tabs on me, he would know when I was alone or not. And, on nights like these, I didn't want to be alone.

"We should head back this way." Nigel pointed down the trail he had traversed earlier.

"Let me check which route is quickest."

I told Stephen I was heading out, and he invited me to the precinct tomorrow morning to review what they had collected. I wasn't allowed to question the girls or Brent, but I could sit in and blend in with the background. He would text me when and confirmed the trail Nigel had suggested may be quickest.

Chapter Nine

I FOUND the hotel easily enough, and Johnny had outdone himself. It was extravagant, and I felt completely under-dressed when I saw the doorman. The valet took my car after handing me my receipt, and the doorman bowed, doffing his hat in greeting. Once I walked through the revolving doors, the shimmering lights and opulent foyer smacked the breath right out of me. The manager walked past and asked if he could assist. Once I closed my mouth and resembled a normal person, I said, "Yes," and followed him to the front desk with Nigel following. I had not expected it to be such a lavish hotel.

I unlocked my cellphone with my thumb and thanked Johnny for the room.

He replied, *Everything is on me, Dana. The girls are safe, and we are preparing for Olivia's funeral. Thank you for doing this for me. My family and I are grateful.*

I'd called him on my way to the hotel to give him the good news. I thought he was going to stop breathing from the excitement. When Johnny was an FBI agent, he was married to a wonderful woman. They had planned on having kids of their own, but, when he was hurt and almost died, he asked for a divorce. He wanted her to be happy and to have kids of her own. She fought him, but he pushed her away and served divorce papers before she could respond. It was noble of him but also sad. She would visit him on occasion and even introduced her newborn to him. Since his divorce, Johnny spoiled his nieces as much as he would if they were his real children. I suspected he and his parents would spoil them with love after this traumatic event. Johnny's family was wealthy, and, even though he was born with a silver spoon in his hand, his parents raised him and his sister with morals and the need to prove their self-worth and not spoiled brats. Johnny wanted to serve and protect, while Olivia was content with raising her children and making a home for herself. She had started a non-profit that fed street children to keep her days busy. They did not make known that they were rich—at all, as if the thought of anyone finding out about their wealth would be a disaster on its own.

The manager handed me my key card, confirming my guest was already in the suite.

I greeted Nigel, and we arranged to meet first thing in the morning.

Once I was inside my suite, the fruit basket on the table boasted nuts, chocolates, dried fruit, a bottle of champagne, and a bottle of water. Against the wall was a small kitch-enette with a variety of snacks, and in the mini bar was more juice and cold drinks. The large bed was soft and smelled of lavender. The bathroom was the size of my bedroom with amenities that shone in the soft glow of the light.

James stood in the middle of the room with his sleeves

rolled to his elbows, the top two buttons undone, and a smile that made me weak in the knees. "Your knight is here, and I brought you your underwear."

I burst out laughing, and it felt so good, especially after the somber day I'd had. "There are people who get arrested for saying words like that." I wrapped my arms around James's neck and kissed him with a fiery passion. His soft lips, warm body, and comforting embrace was what I yearned for. As much as I didn't want to say it, but I was pleased he was here. I had endured a long, sad day, and I would've been miserable without him. "I'm so happy you're here." I moved my arms around his waist and snuggled into his chest.

"Me too." He cupped my face, and our lips touched one more time. When he retracted, he rolled back his injured shoulder to stretch it out.

"Does it still hurt?"

"Only a little." He winked wickedly, picked me up—making me shriek—and carried me to the bedroom.

I FINISHED up in the large marble shower as someone knocked on the door. Pulling the hotel gown tightly against my body, I entered the living area to see a trolley packed with food. My smile reached my eyes. "I'm drooling. The food smells heavenly."

"After all that exercise, I knew you would be starving. I wasn't sure what you wanted, and the food menu was filled with a variety of delicious meals. I picked a handful of items I thought you might like. We have a Chinese prawn dish, burger and fries, sushi, a fruit salad, and ice cream. Not forgetting the bottle of wine." James smiled as he lifted the cloche off each plate to present the various dishes to me. James's smile made him more handsome than he already was; a warmth close to my heart filled me from head to toe. He sat beside me at the table. "What's wrong?"

"Nothing." I must've had a strange look on my face, because he frowned. "Well"—I stood and straddled his waist—"for one thing, I'm glad you didn't get married. Because then"—I kissed his full lips—"I wouldn't have you in my life."

He smiled as our mouths connected again for another lip-lock session. He playfully smacked my ass. When I sat back, he said, "Not as lucky as I am." He caressed the scar on my cheek. Normally, I would've recoiled and covered my face but not with James. He traced the faint scar that, thank heavens, was no longer visible.

The plastic surgeon who removed the pig carving from my cheek was a miracle worker. He had said he was extremely happy with my healing, and nobody would know the difference. Of course, I knew the scar was there. Every time I looked in the mirror, I saw the faint outline of a pig's head as well as the scar running against my jawline. It made my blood boil and the need to catch the sicko that much greater. Not at this moment though; my blood was boiling for other things as the man before me planted soft, delicate kisses on that scar along my jaw.

"Before we do anything again," he said into the nape of my neck, "we need fuel, then I will ravage your body when we're fed."

The plates were clean, the glasses empty, and our stomachs full. I lay in his arms, and we watched a movie that neither of us had seen yet.

"Have you been avoiding telling me about Johnny's

sister, or is there another reason you haven't spoken about it?"

I sat up. "What? No, I'm not avoiding it. It's just …" I sighed. "I don't know. I guess I'm still reeling in the events of the day—lots happened. I don't know." For an hour, I had forgotten about my day because I was with James and I felt guilty for being happy. One thing Dr. Adams kept telling me was I needed to communicate my feelings. I'd felt guilty for not thinking about Johnny and his family, but I still needed to tell James what was going on in my head. I couldn't shut him out when things were going so well between us. "Olivia went camping with the girls, and, from the position of her body and how she was shot, she knew the person. She was found a short distance away from the tent and we suspect she spoke with her attacker where her daughters couldn't hear them." The lines between my eyes deepened. "From the girls frightened faces, they must've seen what happened to their mother. We think they saw enough, and now they're scarred for life."

"What does the lead detective think?"

"He invited me to join him tomorrow again. He's open to show me the evidence they've found, and hopefully, I can sit in when they speak with Brent. I doubt anyone can speak with the girls just yet, but I'll see tomorrow. I think he feels just as guilty as I do for finding Johnny's sister dead and not alive. We all hoped she would be alive."

James pulled me into a hug, kissed the top of my head and spoke near the shell of my ear. "Take it as it comes. This isn't your case. You're only a guest and can only do what you can. It's not your responsibility to solve it, even though you are inclined to do so."

I nodded. He was right, but deep down I felt as though it was my responsibility—I owed it to my friend. I explained how I had come across the skeletal remains and the freak-ishly strange dolls that hung on the branches and the wooden carving that resembled a man meditating.

James rested his chin on my head. "Sounds like a fun walk. Well, I don't know if you would want to return there another time so we can find all the carved men?"

I relaxed in his embrace. "Maybe."

James's cellphone sounded, and he got up to answer it. His face turned a shade redder with tightening around the eyes, and his mouth turned upside down.

What's wrong? I mouthed when he glanced at me.

He didn't answer. When he ended the call, I asked him a second time and louder, only then did he look at me. He placed his cellphone on the bedside table and returned to bed. "Nothing. I need to get up early in the morning."

"Of course." I switched off the TV and the lamp and cuddled into him. "Are you okay?"

"I'm fine. It's nothing, just work stuff. Let's sleep."

James had only been angry in front of me a handful of times. He was generally a very pleasant and placid man and always had his emotions in check. Nothing ruffled his feathers unless it was serious or a bad case. I knew he and Donnie had been working on a case before my missing woman case. And unfortunately, it was something they couldn't discuss with me—and I never pressed him for any information. I didn't want to be one of *those* women who would badger their partner into telling them every single detail. If he wanted to tell me, he would. Until then, I would be there for him.

I squeezed my body against his one last time and slept.

Travis leaned against the wall with one foot up and considered Dafne; she had made an unannounced visit to his home, which he didn't appreciate. "What is it Dafne?" he asked, not worried he sounded cold-hearted.

"I was thinking about the weekend and was wondering what you were up to tonight, that's all." She smiled—he hadn't seen her smile like that in a while—and tucked a loose strand of hair behind her ear.

"What about the weekend?" he asked, still confused as to her presence here late at night and at his home.

"Well ..." She neared and placed her hand on his chest. "We were celebrating, and you asked if I wanted to come over. Do you remember saying that?"

He gripped her hand away from his body and squeezed.

She yelped and tried to back away, but she was still caught in his large hand.

"Dafne, are you off your meds again, because I distinctly remember saying that to everyone. Not just to you." He pushed her away, releasing her hand. He'd had this conversation with her before, and the first time she rejected his offer was a smart move on her part, but now ... now she was taking a chance. "I've told you before, Dafne, you and I won't be a great fit. We will never work. I would use you up and spit you out. Is that what you want? Do you want to be my damaged goods?" He wanted only one person, and Dafne was not *her*. Only one person he would change for, and Dafne was not *her*. He liked nothing about Dafne anymore, other than that she's a quick shot; she never flinched nor hesitated. Her kills were quick and demanding, probably the way she liked to fuck.

"I don't get you, Travis. One moment, you are hot for me; the next, you're cold. I admit, you had quite a bit to drink on Saturday, but you were the one who cornered me. You said I could come over tonight, that we could spend some time alone. That you wanted to be with me." She whispered the last sentence and dusted tears from her face.

Travis chortled. "I think you have me confused with someone else." He shrugged. "Unless you just want a quick fuck and then get out? Nobody ever sleeps over." He won't say, *nobody ever left breathing either*; he liked to take them from behind and choke them—send them off on one last orgasmic high. But he hadn't done that since Eleanor; he was saving himself for *her*.

"Never mind," Dafne said, fastened her coat taut around her waist and headed toward the door.

Travis darted after her, slammed the door closed just as she opened it and gripped her neck. He pushed her against the wall and stared down at her. He leaned in, squeezed her delicate neck and kissed her with a blazing desire he knew would make her dream of him when she was home alone. He pulled away and let her go. "It's best you leave, Dafne. And don't tell anyone about this, for your reputation more than mine." He winked darkly. He opened the door to let her out.

As she walked away from him, he hit her back, causing her to fall forward and crash to the floor.

"And next time I'm that drunk, don't take advantage of me, or you will be the next one I hunt." He slammed the door shut.

As Travis sipped from the tumbler filled with whiskey, his mind raced with what to do next. He remembered drinking at the compound after their hunt and then waking up the following morning with a blinding headache. He remembered the two runners, Razor and Lars, that they were quick to go down, hence the early afternoon celebratory drinks. He remembered all that, but, for the life of him, he didn't remember hitting on Dafne; he would've known if he had. And, for one, he would never hit on her, not again, not after the last time they had shared a connection. He knew it wouldn't work, especially since he was pining for Dana. He chortled at the two names and that they both started with the same letter—a *D*.

The fine thrumming of the music filled his mind, that rhythmic beat he heard when he needed it the most. He sipped his whiskey as he stared at the evening sky. As quickly as the sounds had started, it vanished, followed by a chilled silence. He knew what he had to do with her and possibly the others. Time was running out for the group, and he knew their time together wouldn't last. Sooner or later they would all turn on him, and now was the time he needed to consider cleaning house. He didn't anticipate they would last so long, that one or two of them would've died along the way, nor did he expect it to end so soon. It didn't make sense, but he knew their facades would start to crumble, and he would be left to pick up the pieces and dispose of it.

Travis downed his whiskey and went to his office to replay the tapes. Dana's face filled the screen, and he smiled and sat back in his chair.

Chapter Ten

I WAS one of the first to arrive and stood near the cabin as we waited. Stephen was speaking with the ranger inside the cabin while I sipped on my warm cappuccino.

Stephen came out and smiled. "How are you doing this morning?"

"Good. Miserable weather for a hike." I surveyed my bleak surroundings; the sun was hidden behind gray clouds with rain threatening to drench us.

"Yeah, they say it should clear by lunchtime."

"I hope so." I turned to look up the various paths drowned out by fog.

"The ranger advised us to use this path again today." Stephen pointed to the path we had walked yesterday. "She says this one won't be as affected by the fog as the others, but it will add a half hour to our hike. She will lead the way where we will go off the path and cut through to get to the cordoned-off crime scenes near the campsite."

"Okay." I finished my coffee and threw it in the trashcan.

The ranger closed the cabin door and stood on the path we were about to take. She wore a brown jacket with brown slacks and her hiking boots. She seemed reserved but well-mannered, and I'd only seen her talk to Stephen. I pegged her to be in her late thirties. If she were to wear her hair loose and styled with a little bit of makeup, I was sure she could turn heads. She kept glancing in Stephen's direction, and I wondered whether she had a thing for him. He was a single dad—why not? I smiled at the thought.

Then my stomach dropped as I remembered James and his mysterious phone call last night and wanted to understand what was going on with him but, at the same time, not.

"You ready?" Stephen asked, bringing me out of my daydream.

"Yeah, sure."

More volunteers had arrived, and I walked with them as we followed the ranger. About eight had joined and in total eleven, but the ranger would be leaving us once she escorted us to the crime scenes. The fog was thick and wet against our bodies as we hiked the longer trail. We traversed the winding path, and, as we climbed the mountain, the fog receded but not by much.

Just as I could see the blue sky, the ranger pointed to her left to indicate we had to go through the thick vegetation and deeper into the fog. The grass was tall and the brushes thicker as we snaked through the trees. We followed the ranger first down before going back up the mountain. We crossed over fallen trees or around boulders. The ground was wet underfoot, and, as we climbed over an old stump, someone slipped, bringing one person with him.

Stephen grabbed me out of the way, otherwise I

would've been next. He gripped my elbows so tightly it hurt then he relaxed his hold. "Are you okay?"

"Yeah, I'm fine. Are they okay?"

Stephen went to the two men who had fallen.

One had slipped at such an odd position that his left foot had caught under the dead tree, and the moans from him indicated he had hurt it. Everyone pushed on the stump until it moved off his now-swollen foot, but he could still walk on it. Both men had their asses covered in mud.

We rested for five minutes; the two men who had slipped laughed and plastered their cuts and rinsed their hands in the stream that ran near us, then we continued on.

Not wanting to be taken out again, I followed everyone from the back. I was the only woman apart from the ranger. If any of the men slipped again and landed on me, I would need a stretcher to get out and wasn't looking forward to a hospital trip.

The fog grew denser as we reached a familiar trail and continued toward the cordoned-off area.

Feeling fatigued, I slipped off my backpack and grabbed a protein bar. I ate while I walked and tried not to look at the various doll heads strung high in the trees. It felt like eyes were on me, watching my every move. The hairs on the back of my neck stood, and a shudder ran through me. I finished my bar and tucked the wrapper in my pocket and ran to catch up with everyone. Pulling off my backpack again, I grabbed my water bottle and had a few sips. The half-alert eyes from the heads above were eerily aware, and even though I tried not to look at them, I did. The one closest to me had one blue eye with a twig stuck in the other now-empty socket.

Something moved behind me, and I whipped around to see what it was. Stephen had said the hiking trails were closed to the public and would only open again once it was safe to do so. We were the only ones here, yet I felt another presence. A cool wind cut through the trees, bringing with it more fog that seemed to have shaded the area in a soft gray cloud. Those walking ahead of me blurred as the distance grew between us. Not wanting to be left behind, I quickened my steps until I reached for the person's shoulder to ask them to slow down and grabbed a moss-covered wooden figure.

I flinched, retracting my hand, and glanced around. "Guys? Where are you?" The fog surrounded me. I sucked in deep breaths, and my heart hammered. "Stephen!" The only thing I heard were the sounds of birds flapping their wings and flying away. Movement to my left caught my eye, and I walked in that direction. Then I heard moving water to my right, and I headed there. I was sure I had just passed this tree when I passed it again. I noticed the log on the ground was still there as I climbed over it again. Everything looked the same, or I was going in circles.

I was lost.

No matter where I turned, it was the same trees, the same dead stumps, and the same stream running alongside me. Dread crept into my bones, and I trembled, shutting my eyes. Leaves rustled, and my eyes fluttered open. "Hello?" I called to the man standing in the distance. But it was just another wooden carving. I took my cellphone out my pocket so I could snap a picture and send it to Stephen.

As I aimed my cell in its direction, it was gone. My breath caught in my throat as I lowered my arms and looked where I'd seen the carving, and it had disappeared. It wasn't a carving at all. I unholstered my gun and headed in his direction. Pushing thick tree branches out of my way, I came face to face with a door and pushed it open.

Hands grabbed my wrists and squeezed. I woke, kicking covers off me and hitting James in the face.

"Dana! Dana! Wake up! It's only a dream," James said over and over, trying to pull me into an embrace and hold me down to keep me from hitting him again.

Once I realized I was in bed and not on the mountain, I just lay there, unmoving, to gather my thoughts and to still my heavy breathing. It was only a nightmare. It was just a dream. I was safe. Glancing at my cell, I saw it was almost time to get up.

"You still having nightmares?" James asked in a quiet and gentle tone.

Not having found my voice yet, I nodded and blinked back tears.

He relaxed his grip, and I wiped my eyes dry and sat up.

I exhaled a shaky breath and drank the water I'd left on the side table then laid back down for a few more minutes.

Chapter Eleven

USUALLY AFTER I'D woken after a nightmare and tried to sleep again, that same nightmare would start again at the very same place I clawed myself out to wake up. Instead of trying to sleep after my nightmare, I rested with my eyes open until my nightmare had passed completely. Somewhere between staring at the dark ceiling and counting the various shapes in the room, I'd fallen asleep and awoke with a jolt to a note lying on James's pillow. Only three words graced the piece of paper with his manly cursive handwriting. It brought a smile to my face as I read the words again. *I love you.* I tucked the note into my wallet and sent him a text message filled with emoji hearts and smiley faces. He must've left soon after my nightmare, because I hadn't stirred when he dressed or left.

It was almost seven in the morning by the time I reached the front desk. The tantalizing aroma caught my nose. Near the dining area was a coffee station. I stopped by and asked for a large cappuccino. While I waited for my coffee, I glanced at the guests eating breakfast in the dining room. It seemed to be a popular hotel, as only a few tables weren't occupied. I scanned the guests again, taking my time while I waited, and noted they wore overpriced clothing adorned with expensive jewelry, and a sense of entitlement stifled the surrounding air.

"Here, ma'am." The barista proffered my takeout coffee.

"Thank you." I took the cup from her. I walked toward the exit as the elevator pinged, and Nigel approached but stopped to speak with the receptionist. Someone bumped into me; the sound of boxes hitting my head was the worst that happened.

"Sorry!" someone cried out behind me. "I didn't see you standing there."

I turned to see a woman holding boxes that had almost crashed to the floor.

She had one knee up to help her with a fallen box while balancing the others.

I reached to grab them.

"Don't worry. They're empty, but I still don't want them falling on you."

"Sorry," I said when I realized I was standing in her direct path toward the exit. I sidestepped out of her way. "Can I help you carry them to your car?"

"Nah, it's fine. My van isn't that far."

I read the name on the boxes.

"I make desserts for the hotel." She jerked her chin at a closed door behind us.

"If you made the ice cream I had last night, it was delicious."

"Thanks. And yes, we did make it. I also own the dessert shop on Main Street."

"I might stop by."

"Just ask for Sally, and I'll see if I can put something special together for you."

"I'm Dana, and please don't. I already feel guilty for standing in your way."

"Don't be. It was an accident."

"Ready?" Nigel asked when he neared.

"Yeah," I said. "Nice meeting you, Sally."

"You too." She smiled sweetly, her cerulean eyes creasing at the sides. "Bye." Sally was fortysomething; her skin still held that youthful glow, but her age showed when she smiled.

"Who was that?"

"Someone who bumped into me."

"Come, let's go to the precinct."

I handed my ticket to the valet and watched Sally drive away in her Dodge Caravan with a dessert painted on the side.

Chapter Twelve

NIGEL and I arrived at the precinct just after eight and sat in the waiting area until Stephen could fetch us. We sat in white plastic chairs near the back of the room with the entrance to our right. I heard mumbling and the sound of missteps as someone entered.

The man cleared his throat before speaking to the officer at the front counter.

Glancing at his multicolored flipflops with white socks, I cringed inwardly.

His outfit was mismatched with three-quarter pants and a Hawaiian dress shirt. His hair was neatly combed off his face. His leathery skin shone under the lights, and his eyes glistened with secrets. He whispered to the officer, glanced around and stared at me for a heartbeat then continued in hushed tones. When he was done, he flashed a toothy grin, revealing white crooked teeth.

"Dana?" Stephen pulled me from my strange haze.

Nigel and I stood and followed Stephen to an office he shared with three other detectives. This precinct was the largest I'd ever visited; it had three floors and enough space for everyone. The office we entered had wooden desks on either side of the path and against the wall with each enjoying a window and view of the mountains. The room was clean, but the smell of ink, coffee, and paper wafted in the air. The room was devoid of others, and Stephen led us to the far corner where he'd already started sticking photos on a board.

"Okay ..." Stephen exhaled audibly and ran his fingers through his unbrushed hair. He wore the same shirt as he had yesterday, and the rings around his eyes had darkened. "We kicked up a shit storm yesterday with not only one but two crime scenes and the potential of a third." He pointed to the picture of the hole Dennis had fallen into.

"How is the officer?" I jerked my chin at the picture of the gaping pit.

"He's fine. His shin is full of pins, and he'll be up and about in a month's time. They're still inspecting the hole, along with the cut branches we found near the opening. I doubt we'll find much, so it's going in the *to review* pile for now; we have more urgent matters to address. The skeleton you found is male, but they're still processing him before we can know more. His wallet was missing his identification, and he wore a vintage Fortis watch that showed the day. The watched had a crack, and the date had stopped on the twenty-seventh. This doesn't mean he was killed on the twenty-seventh, because his watch could've continued working after it was struck. And it happened on any month. But, based on his clothing, we surmise he died late nineties, early two thousand. We've pulled a list of missing people over a ten-year period and are currently sifting through that mess because most of it is still paper and hadn't been digitized yet." He took a long sip from his mug. "I know, we should've logged everything, but our old system crashed a few years back, and we had to recapture everything. Unfortunately, some cases, especially the cold cases, weren't." Realizing we were without anything to drink, he asked, "Sorry, do you want some coffee?"

"No thanks," Nigel and I answered simultaneously.

"Right. Now for Olivia." He picked up her file and exhaled an exhausted sigh—no doubt he hadn't slept.

The folder was filled with photographs and reports. Stephen placed them on the desk closest to him. On the board were pictures of the campsite—the bags and strewn clothing in the tent and on the ground, with a few shots of Olivia ranging from distant to close. The bullet wound in her face was messy, and I was grateful the photo was black and white. Her eyes were open, and she had died looking to one side. I perused photos of the ablution facility, the wooden table and wrappers, and then the numbering system marking the evidence on the ground. Arrows pointed the direction of a footprint either coming or leaving the area of the body.

"She was shot point blank in the face, and the ME says she most likely died immediately. He found skin tissue under her fingernails which will be processed, and he will phone me when he has more. All we have at the moment is her campsite. But, before we go there, I spoke with Brent who is at the hospital, waiting to see his daughters. He was with a client the last couple days, and we have confirmed this with his business partner. He isn't a suspect, but we aren't ruling out anything. The girls are in consultation at the hospital, and one of our counselors will be staying with them throughout and giving me an update on their progress." He glanced at his watch. "I think they were both tranquilized when they arrived at the hospital yesterday. Further discussions will take place this afternoon regarding their progress and when we can question them. Right." He paced from one side of the room to the other. "We have Olivia. She knew the owners and had permission to stay at Devil Mountain with the girls during the week. They arrived two days ago, planned to stay for four days and then return home. Olivia always called her mom every day, and, when the evening of the first night she didn't respond, her mom panicked and called the ranger. The ranger had seen them upon arrival, so she knew they were there and inspected the campsite. The ranger said they were the only guests, and, when she didn't see anyone, she called us in. What we found was a messy campsite. I doubt there will be any fingerprints, but we did collect a cigarette butt near her body. Brent says she doesn't smoke, that she detests it and forced him to quit three years ago. She doesn't even drink. It will only be a few days before we'll get her toxicology results back, so I don't know if you still want to hang around here with us until then or go back home until we have more information." Stephen finished by sitting in a chair, a pencil between two fingers, and nervously tapped it on the desk.

"Did Olivia have any enemies?" I doubted she did, but it was something we should consider.

"Her husband says no. She was a stay-at-home mom who ran a non-profit organization. Her worst enemy would most likely be another mom on the PTA, where they would argue over the flavor for the cupcake stand." He slammed the pencil on the desk and stood again. "We are considering a jealous lover, but again"—he rubbed the red stubble on his chin—"most likely not. But we need to consider everything at the moment. Not only Olivia but Brent too. Who knows what happened behind their closed doors?"

With all that I knew about them, Olivia did not look like

the type who would cheat on her husband. But I've learned not to assume anything until we have the evidence backing it up, which we were sorely lacking in this case. Investigating a murder was part waiting, part questioning, part science, and the last part was gut instinct. And my gut told me it wasn't like her to mess around; perhaps she had a stalker she didn't know about. "Did she ever complain about someone following her?"

"I hadn't considered a stalker, but I will follow it up." He wrote something on his notepad.

Now what? We couldn't do anything until we had more evidence, and it wasn't my job to search the crime scenes again. Nor did I think Stephen's captain wanted us anywhere near it. I didn't want to go home and felt I could help with something while I was here. If I couldn't be more involved in Olivia's case, the least I could do was sift through the cold cases for information on our skeleton. At least I would be around if there was a break in Olivia's case.

I glanced in Nigel's direction to see what he thought, but he spoke before I could. "I think I speak for both Dana and I when I say we will be helping in any way you need us. We don't mind looking into the cold cases if it will free some of your officers to assist you on Olivia's case."

"Thanks, that would help us tremendously. It's not something we typically do, you know—bringing in outside help on a case—but you used to be law enforcement. Why not? I'll run it by my captain when I see him. Let me show you to the basement so you can get started."

We grabbed coffee and bottles of water before we descended the gloomy steps into the dusty basement of the precinct belly. Boxes lined one side of the hallway with a room at the far end.

Stephen rambled on how their system had crashed years

ago, and they had to recapture all the case reports again but hadn't gotten around to all of them, hence all the boxes of old case files still littering the basement.

We reached a room in the far back where we met another officer. She had her nose in an old box, complaining each time she got a papercut, then ended it with a sneeze.

Stephen spoke with the officer, and her entire face lit up.

She relocated the box she was browsing through to the large table before us. Dust particles danced in the air, which Nigel and I waved away.

I set my drinks on the table, placed my bag on the floor and pulled out the chair.

The officer lifted out the files with *Unsolved* stamped across them. "Here's the list of missing persons I pulled from the system during those ten years. The actual detail per case wasn't captured because they were so old, but they were logged at a high level so we could still reference them. We didn't lose anything; we just didn't include the detail. All that's here." She tapped the pile of files, wafting more dust into the air.

I waved it away and drank my coffee before I choked on dry particles.

"I'm going to leave you here," Stephen said, stopping in the doorjamb. "Let me know if you find anything." Then he disappeared.

"Okay." I retrieved my laptop from my bag and switched it on. "I'll see if Billie can send us anything on Olivia and Brent. Maybe he can dig a bit deeper than what Stephen and his team could. And perhaps he can narrow down Skeletor for us."

Nigel chuckled into his fist as he rummaged through the

folders with his other hand. He halved them and left a stack beside me.

I struggled to connect to my email or the internet, but I typed the email for Billie, and the moment I received an email, I hit Send. When I was sure the email was out and not stuck in my outbox, I closed the laptop; it was futile trying to do any searches if my connectivity was intermittent, and I hated using my phone—the screen was too small to read on.

I glanced at the list of men who went missing between 1995 and 2005. My stack contained about ten files. I spotted two more boxes filled with more files we still had to check. There had to be an easier way of sorting through stacks of dusty files that could leave papercut and bloodied fingers. Stephen had said our skeleton wore a vintage Fortis watch, and on the wall hung a picture of our guy in his rags with a closeup of the watch. I flipped open the first file and checked to see if he wore a watch. Those with watches I put in one pile, those without went onto another pile. I needed some semblance of order before I wasted time digging into all the details. I told Nigel what I was thinking, and he whisked through his pile and started onto one of the boxes from the floor.

In thirty minutes, we had three piles; the main one was men, where it was confirmed they wore watches, the middle was those who were a maybe—the person who had reported them missing didn't know if they wore a watch or not—and the last was a definite no. We halved the main pile of watch-wearing, missing men between us and finished our coffee—if I drank any more, I would shake—and started on my bottle of water instead.

Again, I wanted to cut the time and only focus on someone who might dress similarly to our skeleton and who was a similar height. The pictures in the files had been relatively recent of the missing person, along with a guesstimate of their heights. Again, I flipped through the files easily enough until I had three piles again.

Nigel had done the same. After an hour, Nigel had twelve files, and I had eleven in which we had to review the detail.

We were so busy we'd forgotten about lunch. After we had acquired a few papercuts and hands full of dust, the same officer entered our little room with a bag. I could feel the heat come off the package as she held it near my face, since this office felt like a fridge. The smell emanating from that bag made me salivate.

She was pleasantly surprised by how quick we had been when I shared what we'd done. She pointed to the janitorial door where we could wash our hands.

We ate our burgers and fries while sifting through the details, noting important facts along the way. It was only when my cellphone pinged with a reminder did I realize it was after five in the afternoon. My eyes burned as I stifled a yawn.

A knock on the doorframe brought our attention to Stephen. "How did it go?" he asked and entered.

I explained what each pile of files represented and tapped the one closest to me. "This pile could be Skeletor."

His brows furrowed at my reference to an old television show.

"Once we know more about him, it could make our lives a little easier. But we've already started going into the details of these missing men. That box over there are unsolved murders." I pointed to the box on the floor; we'd gone through it just to be sure even though none of the names on the files matched the piece of paper on the desk the officer had initially pulled.

"This is great. Hopefully you've narrowed down the correct cases." With one hand on his hip, a smile tugged at the sides. "I've brought you a gift. The ME finally gave us some information. He was in his late thirties or early forties and had brown hair." He handed me another file. "Our Skeletor, as you so kindly renamed him, has a skull fracture, along with broken fingers and a shattered ankle. Whoever killed him had made him suffer, and he most likely died slowly."

"Jesus," Nigel breathed beside me, flipping open the file so we could see the ME's findings.

We had made notes of each of the files so once we had more info on Skeletor, we could easily review then go over the finer details of that case.

"We have five files where the men had brown hair." I retrieved those files and handed Nigel two and gave one to Stephen.

We skimmed through them. The two files I had, the men were in their late fifties, so they didn't match our victim.

"This could be him. Brown hair, forty years old, he has a rap sheet as long as my arm. This has to be him." Stephen read the information with a deep crease forming between his eyes. After a few minutes, he handed me the criminal record.

Eugene Lawrence had been arrested for many reasons: theft, possession of an unlicensed firearm, discharging a weapon in a residential area—the list went on. I stopped at his murder charge. On December 25, 1989, he was charged with killing a couple, leaving a boy orphaned. He only served six years, released on good behavior, and never arrested again until his disappearance.

"We need to speak with his girlfriend." I tapped Delilah's name; she had reported him missing in 2000.

Stephen took the file from me and disappeared.

"Well, that went well." Nigel stood and stretched his long limbs. "It only took us the entire freaking day. Now what?" He stretched his lean body to the left then to the right.

"Let's wait to hear if Stephen can find the girlfriend." I jotted down what we had discovered. When I reread what I had written, my hands shook. The walls seemed to enlarge and shrink, as if breathing. All sides of the small room edged closer as the air thickened, and I breathed in short, shallow breaths. Everything seemed hazy around the edges. I stood, gripped the table to maintain my balance and paced while fanning my face.

"What's wrong?" Nigel asked as he approached.

"Don't touch me," I shooed him away. I couldn't find my voice again, so I pointed to my notes with a shaky finger.

He realized what I was trying to tell him and read what it said. "*Possible vigilante killer, likes to torture, breaks bones, shatters ankle. Check with Johnny regarding—*" The ink had smudged near the end, cutting off the last word. He turned to me. "You think it's Pig-head?"

"I don't know, but it sure sounds like him. We found that biker's body ..." I swallowed hard, the bitter taste of coffee and burger threatening to repeat itself.

"I remember." He nodded. "His right ankle was crushed and duct-taped, and all the bones in his hands were broken. His face looked like it was pummeled in."

I nodded, biting my bottom lip.

Nigel read the ME report again. "His skull was fractured, every finger was broken and a shattered ankle. Yep, the coincidences are too great to ignore. We need to find out all we can about this guy, Dana. I mean everything. If Pighead did this to him, we have a way of discovering who he really is. You know how we've tried to find him. He's a ghost." Nigel took a picture of the report. "I'm asking Billie to send us everything."

Chapter Thirteen

ONCE MY BREATHING HAD STEADIED, I wiped tears off my face. Instinctively, I touched my cheek. I checked my calendar on my phone and saw my appointment with Dr. Adams was this Friday; I didn't have to wait too long to see him. I thought I was okay—I felt as though I was doing okay—but reading through these cases and that we may have another Pig-head victim had brought *something* to the surface. I'd composed myself, and we packed up our belongings; it was almost six in the evening, and James would be staying by me again tonight. We left the files as is; we would most likely return in the morning.

As we ascended the stairs, Stephen was coming down but stopped halfway when he saw us. "We may have a problem." He held up a printed document. "Delilah, the woman who reported Eugene missing, was discovered in her bathtub five days after he went missing."

As much as I wanted to say it was a coincidence, I knew it wasn't. "Was it ruled a suicide?"

"Yep, slit her wrists and drowned." He handed me the

printed report. "I think we may have to take another look at it. Even though I was here when it happened fifteen years ago, I didn't work this case nor remember it." He turned and climbed the steps while we followed. "I don't think this relates to our current case, but there may still be a killer out there."

Deep down, I knew it was Pig-head, but, at the same time, I couldn't be absolutely sure yet, therefore I didn't want to say anything to Stephen until we knew more about Eugene's and Delilah's cases. "We could take a look at it if you want, let you know what we come up with?"

"That would be great, thanks. With you helping us, it's taking a load off our shoulders. I'm heading to the hospital if you want to tag along. The judge signed an exception order to HIPPA allowing us to view the children during questioning. The counselor said we might be able to ask the oldest girl a few questions. She will ask her a few questions first to see how she responds."

———

NIGEL and I stood in a little room with a two-way mirror into pediatrics; the room we had a view into had cartoons painted on the walls, a doll house, a couple of Barbies, plush toys, and a train set. This room was reserved for trauma patients or those who had been abused and needed a safe space to explain to a doctor or psychiatrist what had happened. From what Stephen had said, the psychiatrist and psychologist worked together with the pediatrician to give the young patients the best quality care with the least amount of additional trauma brought on by relaying their experience. And the room we were in was rarely used, as it violated HIPPA, but it was used in special circumstances like ours; we needed to know what the girls had seen to help the case.

Charlotte sat on the floor with her arms wrapped around her bent legs, her chin propped on her knees, and she stared deadpan at the psychiatrist.

The doctor was patient and only asked close-ended questions. "Was it just the three of you camping?"

She nodded.

"Did you hear your mom argue with someone?"

Another nod.

"Did your mom tell you to hide?"

A nod.

"Did you see who did it?"

Charlotte's green eyes glistened like shattered stained glass.

My chin trembled at the sight of her pain, and all I wanted to do was hug her. When one is exposed to any kind of trauma or assault, you relate to the other person's pain.

"Johnny should be arriving soon," Stephen whispered beside me.

I doubted Charlotte could hear us, but the silence in the small room was ear shattering. "He's coming here?"

"Yes, with his parents and full-time nurse. They want to be here for the girls."

"I'll stay until he arrives." I wanted to see him and offer my condolences personally. We spoke habitually once a month, but I would only visit him when I had a chance, since he was out of state. With everything that had happened to me, I hadn't seen him in six months.

"If you saw the person again, would you be able to let us know?" the doctor asked, and Charlotte shrugged. "You're doing fine, Charlotte. We can go slower if you want."

Charlotte nodded, her chin trembled, and tears streamed down her face. "It was so dark, I had to pull Ava backward so she couldn't see. I didn't want her to see what was going on, but we could hear Mom yelling and crying. After the yelling was a scuffle then silence. The silence dragged on, then we heard fighting again. We hid in a ditch behind our tent. I only watched for a short while. I didn't want to see everything." Charlotte buried her face into her lap and cried.

"I think that's enough. Thank you, Charlotte. I was wondering if you could sit with a sketch artist and have them draw the person you saw. Do you think you could manage that? Help us find the person who did this to your mom?"

She nodded.

Brent flew into our room like a bat out of hell, grabbed Stephen's collar and rammed him against the other side of the wall. "I want to see my daughters, Stephen. You can't keep them from me."

Stephen unhooked Brent's fingers from his clothing and pushed him away as Nigel grabbed him from behind and pried him off Stephen. "It's not me, Brent. But, if you carry on, I will lock you up for assaulting an officer. Get a grip and think of your children. They need to first feel safe, and only when the doctors are happy with how they are coping, can you see them."

"They said you were first checking my alibi."

"Yes. Technically, that's correct, but I've done that. Now let the doctors do their thing." Stephen placed a calm hand on Brent's shoulder and gently pushed him out of the room. "Stay out here, let me finish what I need to do, then we can discuss it. But, if you attack me again, I will arrest you."

Brent averted his eyes and left the room.

"What was that all about?"

"I didn't want him telling the kids stories until we had their side first. And we needed to make sure he wasn't at the campsite. His alibi checks out, but I still want to make sure he wasn't there or had hired someone."

"It was a woman," Charlotte blurted as the psychiatrist stood to leave. Charlotte whimpered and buried her face into her knees again.

"Jesus. A woman?" Stephen opened a door that led into the psychiatrist's office, opened the other door and called her. He whispered into her ear.

"Charlotte, are you sure?" the psychiatrist asked after a quick conversation with Stephen. "Can you remember anything about her? Perhaps the color of her hair or eyes."

"She wore a black hoodie, and her eyes looked dark. Sorry, that's all I remember."

"It's fine, take your time. But I still would like someone to listen to your description so they can draw her, however you think she looked like. Do you think you can do that for me?"

Charlotte nodded.

The psychiatrist exited for our room. The lines between her eyes had deepened. "I don't think she should continue answering questions today. I think you got enough to work with for now."

My eyes were drawn to the psychiatrist's name badge— Dr. Crowe.

Stephen nodded. "Thanks, Doc. How is Ava?"

"She only talks to Charlotte and doesn't allow anyone near her. I understand the uncle and grandparents are on their way?"

Stephen nodded.

"I want to give the girls another day before any other

family member sees them. I've asked Charlotte whether she wants to see her dad, and she says no. Call me tomorrow about their progress."

"Thanks, Doc. Let me know if anything changes or if you need anything from us."

"Will do," Dr. Crowe said and left.

We vacated the small room and entered the large hospital corridors where kids were either waiting for treatment or already in their rooms. We headed for the exit.

Stephen sent Johnny a text to let them know what the doctor had said and that it was best they return the following day.

Nigel and I returned to our hotel where we decided to sit in the dining area. James wasn't here yet, and I didn't feel like room service or eating alone, and neither did Nigel. We'd worked together for four years, and this was the most time I'd spent with him in one sitting. He would usually stop by the office in the morning, make his horrible coffee, give me crap about something I was doing or the way I had styled my hair, then leave for the rest of the day. Even though he looked sloppy—like he had fallen out of a bed and didn't bother cleaning himself—he wasn't that bad to be around. I also suspected he was helping me by keeping an eye on me; we hadn't seen Pig-head in four months, and, if he was as determined as he was before, I would be seeing him soon. And if I had shot him, he was healed by now.

Chapter Fourteen

I LIT the candle that stood on the bathtub and poured myself a glass of wine that came with the welcome bundle. The water was hot and left my skin pink as I soaked my aching muscles from sitting in the basement all day. I heard the lock of the door click as James used the keycard he had.

He kissed my cheek upon entering the bathroom. He was speaking to someone on his cellphone, and it sounded like a heated discussion. I would usually leave him—it was part of his job and certain cases I wasn't privy to—but he swore at the person on the other end. This was the second time in two days that whoever was on the other end had upset him.

I finished in the bathroom, dried myself and pulled on one of his clean shirts I'd started wearing as pajamas. I touched his shoulder and mouthed if he was okay.

He kissed my forehead, gave me thumbs up, went into the bathroom and closed the door behind him.

There wasn't much I could do if he didn't want to speak to me about whatever was going on. I padded to the living area where I'd left my notes and laptop and switched it on to check the email Billie had sent me. We'd asked him to give us everything he could on Eugene Lawrence and Delilah Montgomery, as well as Olivia and Brent Newcastle.

Double clicking on the attachment labeled ON and BN, I delved into their lives. As I already knew from meeting Olivia a handful of times, she was a likable person with no shady past. She had rave reviews on her non-profit website, and she hardly had to ask for money, as her connections donated on a regular basis, which meant those she fed got food every single day. She'd facilitated building a homeless shelter where the residents would receive a monthly package containing a bar of soap, washcloth, toothpaste, toothbrush, and deodorant. The shelter was divided into women and children, and men. Olivia worked with social workers to try get them jobs, and, if the statistics were to be believed, fifty-five percent of those who came to her shelter found work within four months. It wasn't easy what she did, but she managed just fine. She was never issued a fine, and the other parents at school seemed to like her as well. She was one of those really good people who gave what she could yet maintained her ground so she wasn't a pushover.

Brent, on the other hand, wasn't as spotless. Before meeting Olivia, Brent was arrested for soliciting a prostitute, and, because it had been his first offense, he paid a fine and had to work forty hours community service at a homeless shelter—that's where he met Olivia. He charmed the pants off her and crept into her life like a leech, where she paid for his business studies and helped him start his business. The more I read about him, the more I wanted another bath. His business grew, and he formed a partnership with another man, Lewis, who had the international connections required to ensure their business made over five million dollars profit the second year. Brent didn't have any other online presence that Billie could see, and I wondered if he had used a different name.

Next, I opened the attachment labeled EL and DM, but there wasn't much—copies of their drivers' licenses, birth certificates, and where they went to school. They were born and raised here near Devil Mountain, and they were high school sweethearts. They had lived together in a small apartment rented under her name and were both dead by the age of forty. In the attachment, Billie had included all of Eugene's arrest reports with the names of his victims. One of them stood out:

Date of incident: 25 December 1989
Case number: WT 12/25/89/3469
Name: Eugene Lawrence
DOB: 02/06/1961
Height: 5 foot 9
Weight: 211 lbs
Incident: Theft, Murder
Reporting officer: Officer Simon Daniels

Incident description: On December 25, Mr. Eugene Lawrence was caught leaving the scene of a robbery and double murder. The only witness to the alleged crimes was a ten-year-old boy who had seen Mr. Lawrence murder his parents for his dad's wallet and mom's wedding ring. Mr. Lawrence claimed he was only walking by when he heard shots and started running in the opposite direction when he saw police. He had priors and didn't think the police would believe his story about being in the wrong place at the wrong time. The eyewitness juvenile was taken to a place of safety where a social worker questioned him. The witness made a positive identification of Mr. Lawrence from a photo array.

I CHECKED the notes I had made on his case; Delilah reported Eugene missing on December 25, 2000. Delilah was found dead in her apartment on December 30, 2000. Either Eugene going missing on the twenty-fifth of December and the double murder taking place on twenty-fifth of December was coincidental or on purpose. My gut screamed that it was intentional. We needed to review the evidence collected from her apartment because I didn't buy her suicide. She went from being concerned about her missing boyfriend to typing a note saying she would rather be dead than live without him. How did she know he was gone and never to return? Unless the person who made Eugene disappear didn't want Delilah making a stink and got rid of her just in case. It was suspicious and needed another look.

We also had to find out what had happened to the little boy. I reviewed the information Billie had sent and the victims for the double murder; Mr. and Mrs. Green. They had a ten-year-old boy named Travis Green which I assumed was the same boy who had positively identified Eugene for their murder. I wanted to perform a quick search to see where Travis was. Upon entering Travis Green's name into the search bar, my laptop pinged and the screen tunneled black until all I saw was his name before it winked out, leaving me with a black screen. I switched it on again, but it was dead. I connected the charger to the wall socket and switched on my laptop to try again. While I waited for it to restart, I leafed through my notes. Once my laptop was on again, I tried searching for Travis's name, but again, the same thing happened—the black screen of death and then it died. Frustrated, I used my phone, and that too died.

When my cell was back on, I texted Billie to let him know what had happened every time I tried to perform a search on the Green family and asked him to send me everything on them as well—the mom, dad, and the little boy and where he was today. The information he had sent with Eugene's arrest reports only detailed their names.

Billie responded with a thumb's up emoji.

Warm fingers curled around my neck, and my arms pebbled.

James came from the side and kissed my temple. "Everything all right?" he asked and sat beside me.

"Everything keeps dying whenever I try to search for this family, so I've asked Billie to help out." I'd told James about Billie and what he did for us. He was fine with us using him. He had heard some good things around the precinct about Billie and what he did for them on occasion. If it solved crimes, he didn't care, just as long as the perpetrator was behind bars in the end and we had the evidence to prove it. "Everything okay?"

"What do you mean?"

"With your phone call. You sounded agitated or something."

"Oh, that. Yeah I'm good."

"You sure? It's the second time I've seen you angry during a phone call."

His demeanor shifted slightly. "It's my old boss. I'm still wrapping up a case that side."

When I realized he wasn't going to elaborate, I didn't push the subject. I asked if he'd eaten, and he had. All he wanted to do was shower and sleep, then he went to the bathroom.

I reviewed my notes, and, when my laptop was on again, I checked my emails.

When James finished showering and entered the bedroom, water glistened off his body as he wrapped a towel around his waist.

I could tell his shoulder still bothered him by the way he walked and tried to stretch it out. I set down my laptop along with my notepad and joined him on the bed. I beckoned him near so I could massage his shoulder. "Maybe you should take a pain killer or a muscle relaxant?" I rubbed his deltoid and trapezius muscles.

"I've already taken a pain killer. I think I just need to rest." He turned to kiss me on my nose. "Your brother and I need to meet up early tomorrow morning, and I want to sleep early. It's almost ten. Let's watch something until we fall asleep."

"Sounds good."

He set the TV timer to switch off after an hour. We watched for a while then fell asleep soon thereafter.

A fine mist surrounded us as we hiked to the two crime scenes—first to the bloody campsite and then where I'd found the skeletal remains. Twenty of us had spread out and searched for the girls. The morning air was cold against my skin, and I could see my breath in front of my face. I'd worn a winter jacket that doubled as a raincoat and blocked the chill. My flashlight was on but dim as it cut through the fog. The mist thickened the deeper I traversed into the thick vegetation up the mountain. The higher I climbed, the colder it got. As we spread out and the farther we hiked, the less I saw of my neighbors or their lights.

I pulled branches out of my way, and the only sounds I heard came from twigs snapping underfoot. My flashlight flickered, and the beam danced across the dark trees, twisting them into sinister styles. When the flashlight winked out, darkness swarmed me. Not knowing where to go, I stopped and took in the gloominess. A twig snapped, echoing around me. I spun around and called out, "Hello?"

A strong black wind blew past me, and I spun around again. The darkness thickened. I hit my flashlight against a tree, and it flickered on. Aiming the light in the direction of the sound revealed nothing. Leaves rustled to my left, and I turned in that direction.

"Dana ..." the wind blew my name softly.

I spun around to the other side. "Hello? Is anybody out there?" Thick darkness filled my vision.

"I see you," the voice whispered, its words caressing my cheek.

Shining the light to the right, I saw someone up ahead. I edged closer and kept my light on them. "Hello?"

"I see you, Dana." The voice was louder and his baritone familiar.

A flash of Pig-head flooded my vision, and my chest heaved as I struggled for air, battling out from the grasp the covers had on me. All I heard was James's voice as he asked if I was okay and reached for me, pulling me into the curve of his body.

Chapter Fifteen

TRAVIS

TRAVIS LEANED FORWARD with his elbows on his desk, his dress shirt straining against his shoulders and biceps. The wound to his shoulder had healed superficially but not completely, and he had to lean back again to stop the throbbing in his joint. After four months, he still couldn't believe she had shot him. He had no idea she was so skilled with her weapon and had hit him in the shoulder, narrowly missing his heart and lung. Aika had to rush him to a friend of hers who had treated him and gave him antibiotics and painkillers.

The red dot flashed on his screen and kept flashing until he pressed ESC on his keyboard to stop the annoying flickering. Using Doe, he performed a reverse search to narrow down who had done it, and the IP address was one he knew off by heart.

"Shit," he muttered, and his ribs pained—or it was his diaphragm; either way, he sucked in a breath and held it until the pain ebbed away. He had been so careful. He'd ensured nobody could trace anything to his family. And anybody performing any kind of search on them would notify him. Now she knew something had happened to his parents, but whether she knew it was *him*, he had to find out. He needed to go there and see for himself *what* exactly she knew.

He sent an email before checking the twenty screens in the cupboard; his company was still his and no other government agency had tried to take it over again. When he had gotten rid of Gregory, his previous partner, nobody had questioned him. Travis had sent postcards from an island in Gregory's name to Gregory's ex, and she had been happy to receive the handsome settlement. The world might think Gregory was relaxing and enjoying retirement, but Travis knew where Gregory's body was buried.

Chapter Sixteen

SOFT LIPS PRESSED against my cheek, followed by, "Morning, sleeping beauty." James's lips found mine, and I opened my eyes when he leaned back on his elbow. "I ordered breakfast. Do you want some coffee?"

"I'd love some. What time is it?" I turned to check my cellphone. "Won't you be late?"

"I'm leaving now, but I wanted to say goodbye before I left." He leaned forward, kissed my cheek and winced as he stood.

"You sure you don't want any painkillers for your shoulder?" I sat on my haunches on the bed and reached for his shoulder so I could massage it.

He sat down again so I could rub it for him. "It's been four months. I don't want to keep taking painkillers."

"If it becomes a problem, you might need treatment again."

"I know. I just don't want to become reliant on them." His cellphone pinged with Donnie's text. "I got to go. See you tonight. Do you have any indication how long you're staying here?"

"Maybe another day, two at the most." I climbed off the bed and followed him to the door. "I want to wrap this up soon. I need my own bed."

"The drive here and back is getting to me, but I can do it for a couple more days."

We shared one last kiss, then he was off, thumb on his phone as he walked toward the elevator. I closed the door, the smell of coffee turning my attention toward the trolley with food.

———

NIGEL READ through Delilah's case report then handed it to me. "I want your impression after you've read it all."

I nodded and took it from him. I read the five pages, then I read it again. "I don't get it?" I stared at the report again, trying to will the words off the page. What wasn't I seeing? The reporting officer had found the deceased in her bathtub, wrists slit, and her body submerged in ruby water. The ME report had stated the facts: water found in the lungs and blood loss due to the gaping wounds in her hacked wrists. As if cutting herself once wasn't enough, she did it repeatedly and on the same spot. And there had been bruising at the base of her skull with an indent at the back of her neck. "He held her underwater. That means she drowned first then bled out."

"Exactly!" Nigel stood and stretched again. He wore the same shirt as yesterday and hadn't bothered brushing his hair. "If it is our Travis Green, he witnessed his parents' double murder. When he's old enough, he seeks out Eugene and tortures him to death and buries him on Devil Mountain. But, when Delilah starts asking questions, he must silence her, makes it look like a suicide. Eugene has a rap sheet and is a known criminal. The police don't care about him. They're happy he's gone. Unfortunately, they would rather use their resources on someone who contributes to society and not takes. They don't care when Eugene is gone, and they care less for the suicide. She too is a nobody that no one will miss." Nigel paced the length of the small room and rubbed the two-week stubble on his chin. "I wonder how many others he has tortured like this?"

"I couldn't perform a search on the Greens. Every time I did, my PC and phone crashed."

"Give me your laptop and phone." Nigel basically sprinted the short distance to me and almost knocked me out of my seat.

"Why? What's wrong?"

"Just give it here."

I handed him my phone, and he did something until it went blank, then he entered some code into it.

"Shit!" He grabbed my laptop and did the same thing. Again, his expression screamed something was wrong and that I should be afraid.

"What is it? You're scaring me."

"You were hacked, Dana. Travis was trying hard to erase his past and that of his family. When someone does a search on them, it notifies him and sends him the IP address of the device that had performed the search. He knows it was you, Dana. He could see the IP address belonged to you."

My body froze to my seat and willed myself to disappear. He knew that I knew. I swallowed hard even though I had nothing to swallow. It felt like sandpaper scrapped down my throat and left a heavy, sinking feeling in my stomach. I felt heavy yet hollow and cold, and I reached for my gun out of instinct. "What should I do?" My voice sounded distant, like I'd left my body as my soul tried to escape what lay before me.

"We need to tell Donnie, Stephen, James … everybody. You need protection, Dana. I know you don't want it, but this time you really do. You know who he is and what he's capable of. And now you know his identity. But he knows too."

"I don't know what he looks like. There's nothing, not even baby pictures. The info Billie sent was sparse—a couple title deeds, including a house here, the name of the company Mr. Green owned was handed-down from genera-tion to generation, and that was it. He couldn't even find Travis's birth certificate."

"If we don't have anything on the Greens, we need to find out all we can on Eugene—where he worked, if he worked, and for whom. He and Delilah went to school here. Maybe we can find old friends who are willing to talk to us. We are the investigators. Let's do our jobs. Snap out of your scared state and do this. I'm with you all the way."

I smiled weakly at him, but I knew he was right. I needed to compose myself and do my job. I should've been happy; I now had a name to the mask.

Chapter Seventeen

WE EXPLAINED our findings to Stephen, and he paled. I could actually see the blood draining from his face and neck. He knew about Pig-head and what he had done to us and understood what type of killer he was. At least Stephen got some sleep, had showered and put on different clothing, but the dark rings around his eyes were evident of another late night. "Are you sure it's *him*?"

"How many Travis Greens do you know? Someone who knows computers and can do what we think he has done?"

Stephen seemed to be fighting with his subconscious about what Travis had done, and I suspected he didn't want to share any of his thoughts with us. I was sure he was slowly coming to grips to what and who Travis really was and what he could do. This was a small town, and, if Stephen had lived here all his life, I was sure he knew about the Greens and what had happened to them—and Travis.

"It's just … It's just—" Stephen stilled as he stared at his PC, then whatever he was thinking hit him like a lightning bolt, and he sat upright in his chair as if the screen had spoken to him. "I remember hearing of his parents' death and what had happened, but I was very young and don't remember the details. It's remained an open case. When I started working here, I didn't think to investigate it, and I didn't even know about Eugene." He pinched the bridge of his nose. "It's sad what happened to the Greens. They were very nice people. I have memories of them coming to this side while on vacation, and they always made an effort for those in need. Shit." He repeated over and over as he typed on his keyboard. "About fourteen years ago, our system crashed. Everything was wiped out. We suspected malware, and the virus spread, making everything unusable. We had to get rid of our hardware, the servers—everything—and start again. It cost the department a small fortune to replace everything, even with the insurance payout. That's when we moved to our current system, and we had to recapture all those old files. We couldn't even do a data transfer, because there was no data to move over. Everything was gone. We hired a few temps to capture the case reports, but we couldn't pay them to finish. That's why most of the old cases are still sitting in boxes in the basement. They only captured the offender's name, their date of arrest, with a short incident report. And, based on the content of the files downstairs, whoever was in these files stole pages before then, when everything was busy being captured." His sigh weighed heavily on his chest.

"You're telling us there's nothing else on your system regarding those cases?"

"No, not that I can find."

"What about Travis Green?"

Stephen arched an eyebrow and paused before responding—again, hesitating to offer us information. "The data transfer I was referring to was through his company.

We partnered with them to help us and provide us with their new software. He even gave us discount." He harrumphed sarcastically. "They developed this system that helps us track, find, and define our targets. All that stuff hackers do, we could do too." He leaned back in his chair, and it squeaked loudly while he scratched the stubble on his chin.

"What's his company called?"

Stephen leaned forward again and moved around the mouse, searching for something. "His company is called Seekster, and the program is Doe. D-O-E, as in John Doe. If I remember correctly, he named it that because his system could find any unknown person intentionally trying to be untraceable."

I cleared my throat, hiding my discomfort. This was how he had found me; he had built a program that intentionally found people. Oh my gods, this was bad. I was in so much trouble ... and now he knew that I knew who he was. He would come after me again and again until one of us was dead. After a few moments, I swallowed hard. "You're saying his program, Doe, can find anyone with a simple search. Yet he has somehow become a ghost, because we can't find him."

He nodded slowly. "Yeah, I guess seeing his parents gunned down at ten messed him up."

"It did more than just mess him up, Stephen. He's a coldblooded killer. He may be the very same Pig-head who killed those other agents and almost Johnny and me, not forgetting the vigilante team of psychopaths he created, who we still haven't caught. They are all still out there, doing who knows what, and we're nowhere near catching them. It's like they've just disappeared." Heat crept up my neck, and my skin tingled. The lack of oxygen made my head light, and my vision fuzzy, and I sat back in the chair.

"I didn't know."

"Nobody did, and I'm sure it was done by design. Travis is a clever SOB. I don't suppose you have a picture of him. I need to know what he looks like."

"No. We didn't even meet him when we contracted with his company. We only met with his business partner, Gregory Johnston." He typed something on his keyboard, frowned and typed again. "Who seems to have retired to Hawaii or something."

"I don't suppose you have *his* picture?"

"This is all I could find." Stephen turned his screen to show me a picture of Gregory.

He had dark almost black hair, with cerulean eyes and a broad smile as he stood among policemen. It looked like the picture was taken with them all in Gregory's office—sleek furniture, wide open windows, expensive statues. On the wall behind Gregory hung a picture of him beside someone on his right, but Gregory was standing in front of the frame, and I couldn't see who it was. On the frame, I managed to read the heading, *Local Company Wins Awards*.

"Does it say what award they won?" I pointed at the picture frame.

"Best startup of two-thousand."

"There's no other picture of Travis? No picture of them winning the award, apart from the one there?"

Stephen shook his head.

"We need to pay a visit to his company then. Where are they?" I stood, ready to bolt before I lost my nerve. "We need to ask them a few questions."

"You can't just go there if he knows you're looking into him."

"I have to go."

Chapter Eighteen

BEFORE HEADING BACK to Chicago to poke our noses around at Seekster, we stopped at the hospital. They were allowing the family to visit with Charlotte and Ava but only on a one-on-one basis. They didn't want the girls to feel overwhelmed, and Stephen wanted to be present.

We entered the children's ward, and I saw his wheelchair first then the nurse beside him. His skin was a pale gray, and he seemed thinner than the last time I'd seen him. He was bound to a wheelchair, with machines to help him breathe. That night, Pig-head had beaten him up so badly he'd broken his neck. He had almost died on the cold road like an animal after being hit by a car. They had resuscitated him on the OR table, but was determined to live. He always came across as grateful for being alive, even though it wasn't what he used to be. He had divorced his wife and told her to find someone who could give her children; it was what she had always wanted. And he didn't think he would live a year, never mind four. He had around-the-clock care who helped him eat, move, bathe, and ensure he could breathe.

I'd seen him in his wheelchair before and had visited a few times, but today felt different. It was incredibly sad, and my breath caught in my throat as I fought back tears. Tears for his sister's death, tears for what he had endured, and tears for the unknown. We'd become closer friends when he was discharged from the facility, and by then, I was a private investigator. At first, I saw him as a mentor who gave me guidance and had introduced Billie to us, but he was also my friend. I wrapped my warm hands around his cold one and watched his face light up from the comfort he would never feel again.

"You made it," he said as the machine helped him breathe with that constant sound of a mechanical lung giving air to someone who should actually be dead.

"Of course. I wanted to say hi and see how you are doing."

"You found the girls, so I'm jumping with joy." He smiled, then his hand twitched. It was only that—a twitch. He would never move on his own ever again. But his body did move involuntarily.

"The team found them, but I'm glad I was there when it happened. We'll find who did this, I promise." I choked on my last word and bit my lip. I hoped to the gods we did. I didn't think I could manage if he or his parents were to pass without knowing what had happened to her.

"Everyone is ready," Stephen said and held the door open to the room we were in yesterday.

We allowed Johnny to enter first with his nurse, then his parents, while we stood at the back and to one side.

Brent sat on a chair and waited for Charlotte. She would see him first, and, if that went well, they would allow Ava to see her dad. Charlotte knew her dad was there.

When the door opened slowly, Brent's face lit up.

Charlotte entered, took one step, then another, but then she stopped. "How could you do it to Mom?" she yelled, blasting her dad with a question that sent all the hair on my body to stand on end.

What just happened?

"It's all your fault!" she yelled and ran from the room.

Stephen almost fell into me, trying to get to the ward where Charlotte was so he could ask her what just happened.

Brent stood with his mouth gaping wide open.

Nigel entered the room and grabbed Brent's arm.

I hadn't seen him move, and he was beside me only a second ago. I asked Johnny's nurse to take the family to get something to drink and would ask Stephen to explain what had just happened. I entered the room Charlotte and Stephen were in, and they were speaking in soft tones. I then entered the larger room where Nigel still held Brent in an iron grip.

"Let go of me," Brent complained, trying to get away.

"What was that about, Brent?"

"I don't have to talk to you."

Nigel released him.

Brent crossed his arms, and Nigel mimicked him, only he looked much scarier than Brent ever would.

Nigel's brown eyes darkened as he scowled at Brent.

Stephen entered and slammed the door. "You lied to us, Brent." He pushed Brent with an index finger. "What really happened that night?"

"I didn't kill her, but I was there. Not at the campsite, I mean, but before they left to go there. The girls were in one booth while Olivia and I were in another. We were just talking."

"About what? You said your relationship was fine, that

you had no problems. You said you still loved her. Which part were you lying about?" Stephen stabbed his finger at him again.

Brent exhaled. "Stop poking me, Detective. There are cameras here, and I will press assault charges against you." He smacked away Stephen's hand. "Okay fine, we were having problems. She wanted to go on this stupid camping trip to *think*. She wasn't happy in our marriage. She wanted to leave me."

"Why?"

"I don't know. That's what we were trying to figure out. Maybe she had a boyfriend. Maybe she was just sick of me. I don't know, okay?"

"What do you get from her estate?"

"What?" Brent shook his head. "Probably nothing. I know she updated her will, leaving most of it to the girls."

"Your lawyer hasn't gotten back to us yet, but I will check with Johnny. What else?" Stephen demanded.

"That's it. We spoke, she wanted to take the girls camping, so I left. She said we would speak about it when she got back, and I left to go to my meeting." He shrugged then sat on the same chair he had sat in previously. "I swear. I didn't kill her." He glanced to his right at his reflection in the mirror and fixed his hair. He was handsome in a rugged kind of way with his neat suit, slick black hair, and blue eyes, but it was an odd time to be concerned about his appearance.

"Maybe you're the one with the lover, Brent," I stated.

He eyed Stephen without glancing my way. "I only answer questions from the police. She's a nobody."

"Fine. I will ask it then. Are you having an affair?"

"No."

Chapter Nineteen

TRAVIS

THE PANIC TRAVIS vowed never to feel again surfaced. The last time he had felt this way, his parents had just been gunned down and were dying at his feet; their blood had pooled beneath their bodies and around his shoes. The man, Eugene, had taken his dad's wallet, his mom's wedding ring, and shot them without blinking an eye. Eugene's face had twitched from whichever drug he had ingested as he pointed his gun at them. But what made it worse was Eugene had worked for their family; Travis's dad had given Eugene another chance—which he had blown right back in their faces, along with the bullets he had shot.

Travis remembered standing in the cold, the sticky blood under his shoes, and his mother's blood on his face and hands. He recalled how his heart had hammered as he stared at the red liquid on his hands and how slick it had felt. Then the helplessness that had followed, that he couldn't help his parents or to stop their deaths; he was only ten. With wide eyes, he had seen their lifeless faces and mouths gaping open, then he had turned to the man who had ruined his life. Eugene had said something he couldn't hear. All he'd seen was Eugene's lips move while his pulse thundered in his ears. It was only when Eugene had shaken him while a smile crept across his face and Travis had heard, *"You are liberated, my boy. Everything is now yours, but I'll see you soon to collect my reward."*

At first, Travis never understood what Eugene had meant, because he was so young, and he'd never seen the man after that day. But, as he got older, he started to remember…

"Close the door, Travis," his father said.

Travis did as instructed and stood with his hands behind his back, averting his eyes as he braced himself for what was coming next.

Crack!

"Count with me, boy."

"One," Travis said through gritted teeth.

Crack!

"Two."

Crack!

"Three!" Travis yelled and bit his bottom lip as the pain shot through his body—one nerve ending at a time.

He counted to ten that day. Ten lashes on his back with a whip his dad used on one of their horses … and now, him. It wasn't so much the pain or the blood. He deserved the lashes. He had broken his mother's favorite vase while playing ball inside the house when she had explicitly said not to. What hurt the most was his mother watched with a malicious smile plastered on her face, almost as if she enjoyed his punishment.

But that wasn't why Travis sought after Eugene. That wasn't why he took out his frustration on his face, broke every bone in his hands, or smashed his ankle. It wasn't why he drowned his girlfriend and savagely slit her wrists.

Travis's dad was away on business and had sought help to fix a few things around the house. The man his dad had hired was dirty and had a scar near his eye, but he was young and strong and watched his mother like a hawk. The man was in the kitchen, painting the walls, when his mother offered him lunch before she even considered giving Travis anything to eat. She wore the long dress she only wore for his dad. She never wore it any other day, only for their anniversaries. Yet, she wore it today, the flowing red dress that accentuated her curves and revealed more skin than he wished to see on his mother.

After lunch, Travis left his plate on the kitchen counter. The painter was nowhere to be seen. He wanted to kick ball outside and entered his room to fetch it. Strange sounds emanated from his parents' bedroom, and the door stood ajar. He slowly opened the door and saw the painter grunting over his mother. He closed the door so quickly it banged against the doorjamb. But nobody came after him when he ran down the stairs and out the front door. Nobody was after him to punish him for entering his parents' bedroom. He should've been happy, but he wasn't.

Travis stayed outside until dark. He wasn't sure if his mother would ask the man to whip him like his dad did. He wasn't sure whether his mother was angry he had seen them. The man finally exited his family home and walked down the driveway, whistling. When he caught sight of Travis sitting under a tree and bathed in shadows, he waved and said, "Catch you later, sport."

From that day, Travis stayed away from his parents as much as he could. He completed his studies and ate his food, but he stayed outside when they were both home. The man returned to finish a few other chores his dad had asked him to do. Whenever Travis did something wrong, he was lashed while the man would watch, like his mother. Only, he didn't have a smirk on his face.

His parents fought more. His dad moved into another room. His mother's belly swelled. His dad decided they would stay at one of their other homes for a few months. His parents were happy again. They laughed. They held hands and went on picnics. Travis wasn't lashed again.

Until his dad found out the date of conception.

Then Christmas came.

And Eugene took away his sister.

He was her big brother no matter who the father was. The helpless feeling and dread Travis had felt when he saw his mother lying in the gutter like trash stayed with him. He knew his sister was not trash and didn't deserve to die like that. And, by the time the paramedics came, she had died before she'd had the chance to live. She was helpless to defend herself, and the people who were supposed to protect her didn't.

That's why he hurt Eugene and his worthless girlfriend. They were trash.

And now … his Dana knew *something* about him. She'd tried to search him. *What did she find out?* Travis had to know what else she knew.

But this was his Dana after all, the same woman who had deciphered his pattern four years ago, the same woman who stood her ground and glared at him, the same woman who, four years later, didn't flinch when he had hurt her again. She would not back down and wouldn't care if she died trying.

He knew she would eventually find him, but he didn't think it would be so soon. But he also thought the same about nobody discovering his pattern four years ago. He didn't think she would figure out that he was dumping the bodies in the shape of the letter *T*.

He had plans for her, and, although he wasn't ready, he would manage. He could accelerate what he had in mind and still do what he had set out to do. But first, he needed to know where she was and what she was doing. One of the little monitors in the cupboard buzzed loudly. There was only one reason why it did that. His program had recognized her face. She was at his company.

Chapter Twenty

WE DROVE to the mansion that once belonged to the Greens. It had been in the family for years until Travis had it sold in 2000, the same year Eugene went missing, putting Travis in the area at the same time as Eugene's disappearance and Delilah's so-called suicide. We parked across the street and stared. The windows and doors were boarded, and the grass was at least knee high. Chains and locks prevented anyone from entering the grounds or the monstrous house. If Travis Green had sold the property, no one lived in it. The documents Billie had sent us stated a closed corporation had bought the house, and that's where the trail ran cold. There were no neighbors for at least a mile on either side, and it didn't look like anybody had been here in a very long time. We didn't bother getting out to walk around the property; instead, I made notes, then Nigel drove us to the next address.

The apartment where Eugene and Delilah had lived fifteen years ago was on the second floor and now occupied. The area had deteriorated over the years from lack of upkeep. Papers littered the ground, along with the stench of urine. Men sat near the entrance and stared at us. One of them used a switchblade to clean his nails.

"I've seen enough. Let's go to Seekster."

Nigel drove the three hours to downtown Chicago where Travis Green's company, Seekster, was based. It was a tech startup from the late nineties, which he had started when he was nineteen or twenty. What his company did back in those days was at the head of the curve and had sought many contracts from the government. But that's all we knew about it. Again, Billie could only scrape the top of the surface—which wasn't much. The developers working at Seekster were good, and Billie couldn't get much on the company or the employees. It was no wonder the government wanted to work with them; nobody could investigate them—how ironic. But they were listed, and we could visit them. They also offered private packages for individuals, but what those packages were, we had no idea.

We parked in the basement in the visitor section and took the elevator to reception. All the glass caused the building to glisten like a star from the outside. Inside, they employed enough armed security for Fort Knox. We had view of the reception desk and a turnstile where employees gained access via their retinal scanner. That was it. Something was unsettling about the sterile building. There was no personal touch or that welcome, homey feeling.

A man with neatly gelled hair greeted us and asked who we wanted to see.

We told him we wanted to see the person in charge.

The poor guy almost crapped himself as he stammered —unsure of what to do next. It was as if nobody had ever asked him to see the boss. "Uh, Mr. Green only comes to the office for important business, but he's never far. If you'd like, I can arrange a teleconference with him." Beads of sweat peppered his forehead.

"That's fine. We don't mind. We only have a few questions, then we'll be on our way."

The receptionist turned to face the wall behind him and whispered into his phone. When he was done, he said we could wait over there and pointed at the seats in the corner.

We waited an hour before anyone approached us. We stood when she stopped near us.

She was as tall as me, lean yet curvy, with long raven-colored hair and light blue eyes. "Hi," she said with an outstretched hand. "My name is Aika. Mr. Green isn't here, but I would gladly answer any questions you may have." She shook Nigel's hand first, then, when she shook mine, one side of her mouth curved upward in an awkward smile only I could see.

I ignored it for now.

A security officer gave us access through the visitor's turnstile. We followed Aika to the elevator then rode to the tenth floor.

"The company has grown over the last four years." Aika broke the silence. When she said four, she glanced at me.

My palms sweated, and an ice-cold breeze caressed my skin, almost as if she had said it on purpose like *that*. I couldn't help but wonder if she was part of his killing team. I made a mental note to ask Billie to investigate her.

I ignored her remark while Nigel responded, "What happened four years ago?"

"The previous general manager retired. We think he was holding the company back from lucrative contracts. But, since he's retired, the company has had the most contracts we've had in years." Her smile was malicious and way too perfect.

We entered a small meeting room where cappuccinos waited for us in the middle with three croissants on a plate. We sat, and Aika offered us a coffee each and pushed the croissants our way. Something told me not to touch anything that came from this company. Pig-head, which I now knew was Travis Green, had roofied me and carved his pig-head into my cheek. The last thing I wanted was another dose of drugs and to be stuck in a room with him, or her. I just smiled.

"Right. What can I help you with?"

"Can you tell us about the various contracts your company has?"

"It's classified. If I tell you, I'd have to kill you." She snorted. "Seriously though, I can't say anything about that, but what I can tell you is it's with the various government enforcement agencies. I just can't divulge the details."

"Can you tell us anything about what your company does?" Even though we had an idea, I was hoping to get a direct answer from her.

She thought about it. Her hand found her mouth as she carefully considered her words. "Data. We perform various searches, and we assist the police."

"We're investigating a murder near Devil Mountain, and we came across skeletal remains which we think may be linked to the company. We wanted to ask Travis whether he had heard of this man so we could rule out the company." We knew Travis already had the company in 2000. If we asked the questions this way, it would look like we thought Eugene was an employee or somehow linked to the company and not directly to Travis or his family. We weren't accusing Travis of anything, yet. We were only asking questions.

"Can you give me the name of the person so I can find

out? Perhaps give me your business card, and I can get back to you?" Her lips twitched.

I wondered if she was uncomfortable, not knowing everything. "Sure. Could you ask Travis about Eugene Lawrence from fifteen years ago? Oh, and about the data transfer that didn't happen due to missing reports in Devil Mountain?" I was playing with fire, nudging a sleeping cobra and running before it could strike. By asking these questions, I was telling Travis I knew something but not enough to have him arrested. There were some things he couldn't delete, and now that we had found something, we would be asking more questions, along with the police. What I didn't know was how far up the chain of command Travis could reach and still come out smelling like roses.

"Alright, I can ask him that," she said as she wrote it down.

"Give him my details." Nigel handed her one of his business cards. "I'll be taking over the case, as she will be going overseas soon," he lied.

"Sure." She held the card in her delicate hands.

We left soon thereafter, no point staying if we couldn't speak to someone who knew Eugene. We drove to the office and spoke with Marc. He was busy with property fraud, working with a lawyer and a forensic accountant. I was so bored from the story I fell asleep at my desk.

Marc threw paper clips at my face to wake me.

We checked our emails, listened to voice messages from our landlines and returned any calls. Then we headed back to Devil Mountain. I wanted to find out if Eugene still had any friends in town.

Chapter Twenty-One

NOT KNOWING WHERE TO START, we drove down Main Street, looking for a shop that seemed the oldest and may have been open the same time Eugene was alive and may have heard of him. We grabbed the closest parking spot we could find and walked toward the corner convenience store. The graphics on the outside window seemed like the originals from the eighties.

A man sat behind the counter and was old enough to have maybe heard about Eugene or possibly what had happened to the Greens.

Nigel made friendly chitchat, learning the man liked to be called Dex, then asked the question we were really here for. "Do you remember a man named Eugene Lawrence from about two-thousand—"

"He was a nasty sonofabitch, I tell ya." Dex smiled and turned to stock the cigarette shelf. "He was locked up so many times I lost count. He even stole from this store. He sure had a sweet lady, and I was sad she killed herself over someone, as useless as he was. Not sure what happened to ole Eugene though. Maybe he done some things he wasn't supposed to and got himself in trouble with the wrong folk."

"I don't suppose you remember the Greens?" I asked.

"Yes, I remember them. They were quiet folk and real nice, you know. They came up here once in a while and liked to hike that mountain. They always bought their groceries from me. But their boy was strange though."

"Oh? Can you elaborate?"

"I dunno. Can't put my finger on it, I could only feel it. Like he needed a good whipping to make him right. Anyway, he was way too quiet for my taste. Quiet kids like that is up to no good. They used to go there often." He pointed an arthritic finger at the ice cream parlor across the street. "Almost every single day when they visited our town."

IT WAS ALMOST six in the evening, and I hadn't eaten all day. A knot had formed in my stomach since finding Eugene's remains and hadn't let up. That knot seemed to tighten its grip on me after our trip to Travis's company, and now I had time to think about it, it may not have been the best idea. Soon Travis will realize we were investigating *him* and not only Eugene.

We found an open booth near the back of the ice cream parlor and waited to be served. The menu boasted desserts, savory pancakes, and croissants. Glancing at my options, I decided on a waffle, milkshake, and a cup of coffee.

Nigel picked up a used toothpick from the table and played with it between his teeth. I shuddered at the thought.

"That's disgusting, Nigel."

"What?" He shrugged as he stared hungrily at the waitress as she handed the menu to him. As she was about to leave with only my order, Nigel caught her wrist while glancing at his choices. "Don't disappear, darlin'," he said with a southern twang—"I want the savory pancakes and a black coffee, honey"—and handed back the menu.

The waitress blushed and dashed to the front counter to place our order.

"Aren't you too old to flirt? She's half your age."

"How do you know how old I am? And besides, I come with experience. And I'm gentle." He growled playfully.

"Ugh, I don't want to hear about it."

We discussed our notes from our visit to Seekster, and, in no time, the waitress brought our order. The heavenly sweet aroma from my waffle made me salivate, and the knot in my gut released somewhat.

When she placed Nigel's in front of him, he winked at her, and she blushed again then turned to go behind the counter where she assisted a customer who wanted to pay. She kept glancing at him.

"I wouldn't have believed it if I hadn't seen it with my own eyes, but I think she likes you," I teased.

"How else do you think we'll get information?" He smirked.

"I doubt she'd be old enough to remember Eugene."

"But she'll have parents who were." He shoved a forkful of pancake into his mouth.

My waffle was light and crispy and the ice cream creamy; the entire package was delicious, and I gobbled it up. The knot in my stomach eased, and I felt normal for about five minutes until my cellphone pinged. Billie said he would keep digging and send us information when he found it. I switched on my laptop and read what he sent. "Okay, we have more info on Eugene. He was an orphan, born and lived in this area his whole life. He stayed in various homes, and, like so many others, he never stayed in one for long. Besides the murder charge, he had one other conviction for theft and had served six months. He was picked up for a list of offenses, but we already knew that. He also held odd jobs, tending to gardens or general handiwork, and one of the places he worked at was the Greens."

"That's the connection. He worked for them. He wanted what they had. It was a window of opportunity. But what I don't understand is, why bite the hand that feeds you?" Nigel shook his head. "He could've milked them for what they had and for as long as he wanted. Maybe steal here and there, but he could keep coming back. Why kill them? And why let the boy live? It doesn't make any sense." Nigel smacked his lips while he spoke and ate at the same time. "We need to know more about the Greens. Yep, there's definitely more to this story." Nigel shoveled more pancake into his mouth while I scoured through what Billie had sent us.

"The rest of it we already know. Eugene goes missing on Christmas day in two thousand." I opened the attachment labeled *Delilah*. "The girlfriend was found deceased the day before New Year's Eve, five days after reporting her boyfriend missing. She and Eugene were together since they were both sixteen yet never married. They were both forty when they died. Delilah had a steady job as an office clerk and earned the minimum wage, and the apartment they shared was in her name." Ever since we left Seekster, my mind was fixated on Travis—who he really was and what made him tick. I'd formulated my own profile on Travis, but since I'd never worked a case with Nigel before, I wanted to know what he thought before coming to a conclusion. I wanted to understand Nigel a little better besides just being a colleague. I wanted to know what made him tick, apart from the fact he always smelled like cigarettes yet I'd never seen him smoke, and he always looked like he had fallen out of a dumpster. I had to know what was going on in that head of his; perhaps he had some additional insights. "With everything we already know, what are your thoughts on Travis?"

Nigel finished his pancakes and sipped his coffee, his pinkie finger extending while deep in thought. I'd never noticed him do that before. It was a sophisticated action, yet coming from him, it seemed off, especially since his attire didn't match. "I've been thinking about his obsession with you, whatever else had happened to him from when he was a kid witnessing his parents murder till adulthood. He's about thirty-five years old now, most likely ass deep in the family jewels." Nigel snickered at his comment. "That means he doesn't have a normal nine-to-five job and has a lot of free time and is most likely mobile. He owns and manages his company from wherever he may be. He doesn't have to stay in one spot, which, in my opinion, makes him dangerous and highly unpredictable. Therefore, he doesn't follow any rules. He makes them up as he goes along. I doubt he dabbles in women, drugs, or gambling. But what are his weaknesses? Perhaps he is meticulous, a neat freak with OCD. He prefers order, and, from what he did to Delilah, he plans well, yet violently messy. But that was long ago, and he has improved since. I mean, look at his vigilantism of four years ago with five other individuals and the way in which they killed their victims. The aggression and brutality tells me they are a very special group of people who really love what they do. And how did Travis find them? It's not like there's a group on social media for serial killers. Unless he conditioned them. Anyway, those are my thoughts."

I nodded my agreement. I too had thought the same. Yet hearing the words come out of Nigel's mouth made it all too real and true. My body trembled as I tried to expel memories of the attacks. That Pig-head—or rather, Travis—held the power in his hands. He had a way of coming after me without me even knowing. He was wealthy and therefore had more at his disposal than I could ever dream of. That knot I thought had left twisted its way back, and an ache blossomed under my diaphragm. What would this mean for me in the long run? His obsession would turn deadlier. And, as much as I wanted to hide, I needed to face this, or it would never end. I did not want to constantly look over my shoulder and wonder whether he was watching my every move. And he did not like James. He'd attempted to kill James once before; he would most likely do it again.

Something outside caught my eye. When I looked up, all I saw was the tail end of a coat billowing behind the person as they passed the parlor.

"You okay?" Nigel asked. "You look a little pale."

"I'm fine. It's just my blood sugar," I lied and had another piece of my waffle. My hunger had dipped as I pushed the remainder of the waffle around on my plate.

Nigel leaned on the table as he stood. "Let me speak with the cute waitress, then we should check in with Stephen."

I watched the exchange between Nigel and the cute waitress while I finished my coffee.

He glanced at me and motioned with his head for me to join them.

"Private investigators?" I heard her say as I approached. "Neat. I'd always wanted to be one, you know."

"Do you remember them at all?" Nigel asked.

Before, I hadn't really paid her much attention, but I now studied her carefully. She looked a little ridiculous in her puffy-sleeved, milky-white dress and blue apron. She looked like a milkmaid, and it suited the place. Crow's feet spread on the outer edges of her tired eyes when she smiled —the only signs that she was old enough to speak with Nigel.

"I remember the Greens." She hesitated as she glanced at the entrance. "They were a very nice family. I remember they enjoyed hiking up Devil Mountain. They had a house here and would vacation or come for a weekend. But, when Travis got older and received his parents' estate, he sold the house. He came inside and bought an ice cream ... and actually sat in the same chair you were sitting." She pointed at the booth where we had been sitting.

"Can you remember when that was?"

"About fifteen years ago, around Christmas time."

"How old were you then? That was a long time to remember."

She blushed. "I was twelve and worked here after school. I was very tall for my age," she added quickly. "The only reason I remember him is because of his family, and he's hot. He'd never spoken to me before that day. He flirted with me a little, but then he left abruptly. I think that's why I remember that day so clearly. We were talking one minute, the next, he just got up, threw way too much money on the table and ran out like he was trying to catch up with some-one." She shrugged. "He didn't return, or at least on a day when I was working."

"I don't suppose you remember what he looks like?"

Her cheeks blossomed a healthy shade of pink. "He's tall, has dark brown hair, green eyes, and a nice smile. He makes you feel like you're the only one in the room." She glanced in Nigel's direction then averted her eyes.

I made notes in my book and thought of something else. "I don't suppose you remember him having any scars on his face? Or could you see any tattoos?"

"No, I didn't see any. He wore nice clothing though. I couldn't tell from where, just that it was quality." Her cheeks reddened again. Shaking her head, she glanced over her shoulder at the entrance again. She straightened her apron and headed to the back. As she passed me, someone entered the parlor.

"Annabelle?" the woman yelled so loud it made me jump.

I recognized her as the woman I had met at the hotel. Her name was Sarah, or something with an S.

She remembered me and smiled. "Dana, right?"

"Yes. Sorry, I've forgotten your name." I sounded like the worst private investigator ever, not remembering a name.

"Sally."

"You make desserts for hotels. Do you own this ice cream parlor?"

Her smile reached her eyes, and it brightened her face. "Yes, this is my pride and joy." She turned her attention to Annabelle who was now in the back kitchen. "Well, she's my pride and joy. This pays the rent." She pointed to the ceiling.

"Well, the waffles are delicious. I think it's one of the best I've had in a long time."

"Thank you. That really means a lot."

Annabelle came out from the back. "Hi, Mom."

"Well, it was nice to see you again, Dana." Then to her daughter, she said, "Can I talk to you quickly?"

Annabelle nodded hesitantly. Her gaze flitted to me, then she turned around, with Sally following her.

"Would you mind if we paid first?" I asked, not wanting to wait for them to finish their conversation.

"It's on the house," Sally said.

"Thanks."

As we exited, I could hear Sally yell at Annabelle.

Chapter Twenty-Two

AFTER THIS MORNING'S revelation that Brent had seen Olivia and the girls before they went camping, Stephen had asked him to come to the station to give his statement. He was still at the station and still being questioned. He looked worse for wear; his usually perfect dark hair was sticking in all directions, and dark circles highlighted his exhaustion. He had an old scar above his left eye that, if it was a few millimeters to the left, the original injury would've hurt his eye. He looked a bit pale for someone with olive skin, making his blue eyes shimmer in the sterile light. Stephen had most likely given him enough coffee to keep him awake and jittery, not a great combination if you were under suspicion.

Inside the meeting room with Brent was another officer who stood against the opposite wall with his arms crossed over his large chest. The dark imposing figure loomed over Brent, and I was sure he felt as uncomfortable as they both looked.

"We have to let him go." Stephen pointed at Brent on

the small screen in the CID observation room. "We found scratches on his chest, which we suspect Olivia did while they were so-called talking. They're still processing the evidence from under her fingernails, which, after the rush we put on it, we should get the results soon. We've visited the place where they had waffles before going on their camping trip. And the woman who works there confirmed his story. She did add that it appeared as though they were fighting, and it ended with Brent leaving, spinning the wheels of his car as he left. Then Olivia finished lunch with the girls, paid and left. That's the last anyone saw of them, apart from the ranger when they entered Devil Mountain." Stephen read from his notes then focused on the screen.

"I don't suppose they were at the ice cream parlor on Main Street?"

"Actually, they were. How did you know?"

"We just came from there, and their waffles are to die for." Realizing my choice of words, I continued rambling on, hoping nobody had noticed. "We first went to the convenience store and spoke with Dex who gave us some insight into Eugene, but we already knew most of it. But he did tell us the Greens went to the parlor often when they were in the area. Annabelle said she spoke with Travis when he was last here."

"You don't say. They are one of the places that's been around since my childhood. There's a sad story that goes with the parlor though. What else did they say?"

"She gave us a short description of what he looked like back then. I was amazed she remembered from fifteen years ago, but he sounded unforgettable." I read the description she had given us, and Stephen shook his head.

"That could be anyone."

"I know, but it's a start. If I see any tall men with dark

hair and green eyes, I know to walk in the opposite direction."

"That's not the correct way to live. We have to be smarter." I sighed audibly; I had no idea how to do this.

Stephen cleared his throat and opened the door. "I'm going to release Mr. Newcastle. Do you have any further questions you think I should ask him?"

I couldn't think of any. I shook my head and so did Nigel.

We watched Brent leave the station and climb into a taxi to take him to the hospital to fetch his car. That's what he'd said as he left.

James sent me a text as we descended the stairs. *Working late, see you around ten.*

"Hotel?" Nigel asked as we climbed into the car.

"Yeah," I said, but the tone in my voice sounded pathetic. Perhaps I was just exhausted. "Would you like to have dinner with me?" I asked as I stared out the window, watching the other cars pass us.

"Are you asking me on a date?" Nigel chirped with a hint of humor.

I glared at him. "James will be late, and I don't feel like sitting alone in my suite until he arrives."

"Of course, cupcake."

Chapter Twenty-Three

TRAVIS

HE FELT MISERABLE. Control was slipping through his fingertips. He needed to get his head back in the game. Not only had Dana searched for his name, but she and the other PI had arrived at his company, looking for him. He'd given Aika an assistant position at Seekster to keep her busy during the day and to assist him where required; he trusted her. He knew she wouldn't fuck up things, because she had just as much to lose as him. When the front reception had contacted him to let him know someone was asking for him, he asked Aika to approach with caution.

On one of his screens, when he saw Dana enter the small boardroom first with that other man close behind her, Travis's hands bunched into fists. He relaxed when he heard her voice. It was as delicate and sweet like it usually was. He missed hearing her words. He touched the screen with the tip of his index finger and wished it was her face beneath his fingers, and, as much as he wanted to be there, to smell her skin, he knew he couldn't risk it. He couldn't risk his identity.

The questions she asked made him send his fist into the wall, bruising his knuckles. They had found Eugene, along with the police report he thought he had destroyed.

Now he was driving the three hours to Devil Mountain to find her and get what he had left behind. He needed to fix what was happening or bite the bullet to get close to her. He had left her alone for far too long, and it was time. Her room had been ready for four years already, and his compound was finally prepared for her arrival. It was time for him to take what was rightfully his.

Chapter Twenty-Four

"I THINK that was the best fish dish I've ever eaten." Nigel patted his stomach for added emphasis.

"My chicken wasn't too bad either." I sipped from my wine glass.

Patrons didn't have to stay at the hotel to enjoy the fine cuisine dining filled the dining room. The chef was someone famous and had studied in France before making Devil Mountain his home.

The wine was similar to what James had ordered on our first dinner together. When I saw it on the menu, I ordered it and almost choked when I saw the price tag. But Nigel said he was paying and didn't mind, just as long as the wine was good—which it was.

"How long are you going to be my bodyguard?" I asked after the waiter removed our plates.

"Until we catch him, I suppose. I don't like it any more than you do. Until then, you're stuck with someone."

I'd never heard of Nigel speak of a family nor had I ever asked. I knew almost everything there was to know about Marc, but Nigel was sort of an enigma. "Doesn't you wife or family mind that you're out here babysitting me?"

He stared at me over the rim of his wine glass for an uncomfortable length of time and sipped slowly. "My family died a few years back. It's only me."

"I'm sorry. I had no idea."

"Marc never told you?"

I shook my head.

"It's one of those things, I suppose. I had a wife and two boys."

"What happened?"

"Something I wish daily I could've prevented. I can't change the past, but, if I can prevent your death, then I will die a happy man."

I had no idea of this tragedy and wondered why Marc had never said anything to me about it. It was awful what he'd lost, and no words could ever comfort him.

"I'm sorry—" was all I could say.

"Babe." James's voice boomed over the low hum of the dining room as he approached. He kissed my cheek and sat beside me.

"James." Nigel nodded in greeting.

"Nigel, how's everything?" he asked after kissing me.

"Good. I guess your shift is next. Look after our young friend here." Nigel tipped his head in my direction. "I'll be going." He stood and downed the rest of his wine. "I'll pay for our meal. You two love birds get some sleep, and I'll see you tomorrow morning."

"Goodnight," James and I said at the same time.

"Everything okay?" James asked as he sat closer, his larger hands enveloping mine.

"Uh-huh." I gave him a short version of what had happened during the day.

James whistled low. "Now I know why Nigel said what he did. He's usually the first one to disappear into the night. And you say there's nothing on this guy?"

I shook my head. "Stephen checked on their system, and what Billie sent wasn't much either. Travis ensured he and his family were ghosts and hard to track down."

"I'll be the first to say I don't like this, Dana, I really don't. If Pig-head, Travis, whatever his name is, knows you're looking into him, you are in danger. Does Johnny have contacts into the witness protection program?"

I sighed. I was too exhausted to argue. "I don't want to talk about it anymore. All I want to do is climb into bed with you."

Chapter Twenty-Five

TRAVIS

NOT KNOWING where to look for her, Travis started at Devil Mountain, where he had left the useless piece of shit who had ruined his life. He remembered the cold look in Eugene's eyes as he killed his father first then his defenseless mother—then the slow creep of a smile that knocked the nail in his coffin. Just before Eugene had left Travis standing in a pool of his mother's blood, he had the audacity to wink at him. To wink!

When Travis was old enough, wise enough, and prepared, he'd sought after the best teachers in weaponry, martial arts, and swordsmanship. He even found a master who helped him use the katana, but blades were not practical in today's world and not something he could carry on his person. But he did keep one at his compound.

It was December 25, 2000. Travis went to the one place he knew he could count on to get any kind of information—the ice cream parlor. The bitches who worked here loved to talk about their fellow neighbors, and they did not disappoint. Annabelle had told him Eugene frequented the area every day, and, when he walked past the shop, it was his chance to grab him. Travis put his arm around Eugene, who didn't recognize him at first, but, when Travis smiled and called him Sport, *Eugene knew who Travis was.*

Travis parked his vehicle on a side road near Devil Mountain. It was an entrance he'd used many times before. He didn't want to risk getting caught at the main entrance, especially since it was most likely a crime scene and cops were everywhere. He arrived at a fenced-off area, and the hole was still there. After all these years, nobody had ever come to close it. He traversed through thick vegetation, over a stream, and arrived at one of the carvings; this one was sitting on a tree with its elbows on its knees, thinking. He brushed debris from its head and pulled low branches that obscured its view. Up ahead was one of the trails that was mostly used, but he didn't use it. He cut across the trail, hiked up the mountain and climbed over rocks until he came to a high point where he could see the commotion below. A gaping hole was in the ground where he had left Eugene to rot, with police tape surrounding the area. There was an item he needed, which he would retrieve once nobody else was around. Travis followed an overgrown trail to the campsite where the area was like a bee's nest. He wanted to know what had happened here and how they had discovered Eugene's remains.

Travis retrieved his laptop from his backpack and, using a backdoor connection to the closest police station, found the police report. He sat on deadwood and read through the information and the pieces of evidence collected. *It's the husband, assholes!* He cursed under his breath; it was as plain as day. This was the work of the husband. If he didn't do it himself, he had hired someone to do it for him. And the only way he could find out for sure was if he investigated it himself. But Travis didn't understand why he cared or why he wanted to help. This wasn't something he did. He didn't care, and he didn't want to help. Usually the perpetrators were already found guilty and then released into society, which was an open invitation to him and his team. Yet, he found himself caring and wanting to solve this murder. The only thing he could surmise was perhaps it was because Dana was working on the case. Perhaps it was his subconscious mind egging him on to help her, and it was a way for him to be closer to her, to imagine what it would be like to work with her side by side as colleagues or even as lovers. Travis shivered at the thought of feeling her skin beneath his. He could make the bad things right and make amends for what he had done to her. Again, why did he care? The more he thought about it, the more he realized he did care. He wanted to help her solve this case. He shuddered at the thought. He understood he had hurt her so she would notice him. And the only way he could show her was to do what he had done. He didn't know any other way.

Travis sat there, contemplating whether he would tell her he had assisted her or let her believe she had done it on her own. He smiled at that. He would think about that.

Travis performed a search on Doe, looking into Brent and Olivia and who exactly they were. Olivia did not have any social media, but her non-profit organization did, and that was all above board. Olivia was a gentle soul, from what he read. Brent, however, was on all social media platforms and even a few dating sites but under an alias, and he had various email addresses linked to his IP address. Travis tsk-ed as he wormed his way into Brent's machine, mirroring it so he had sight of everything. The security Brent had installed on his laptop was incredibly weak, and Travis made a mental note to message the company to offer a service Seekster had recently developed.

Travis's laptop made the satisfactory ping sound after the Doe search. *Well, well, well, what do we have here?* Travis opened the folder to see the agent he had maliciously attacked four years ago was Olivia's brother. No wonder Dana was here; she was helping her old direct report.

Travis considered his options—either leave the case as is or help Dana solve the mystery. He knew in his bones it was the husband. Now all he had to do was prove it. He could take a couple days and nudge Dana in the right direction. Sooner or later, she would know who he was. Why not be the one to do it and present her with a gift as well?

Chapter Twenty-Six

I HANDED Johnny's nurse her cup of coffee and sipped from the polystyrene cup in my hand. The coffee wasn't bad here, but it wasn't great either. Johnny's mom was whispering to Charlotte and Ava, and the two girls smiled. Their grandfather added his two cents, and the three women laughed. It was a pleasant sight to witness, and I was relieved the girls would be okay—in time. They had the right support system, with tons of love.

Johnny had already spoken with the girls early this morning before we had arrived, and they had already started to come out of their shells and behave like they had before their traumatic ordeal. Brent, on the other hand, was nowhere to be seen.

"Charlotte said she doesn't want to see her dad and asked if they could stay by me." The machine connected to Johnny's body made a noise, and his lungs filled with air. When he had enough air, he continued speaking. "Unfortunately, my place isn't big enough, but"—the machine breathed—"they will stay with my parents for a while."—

Breathe— "I don't know if Brent is involved in Olivia's death, but something else"—breathe—"is going on that Charlotte doesn't want to say"—breathe—"or is too afraid to say anything."

"Don't worry. We'll find out what it is." I patted his cool hand. A text message came through from Stephen telling me Brent was at the station again. I relayed the message and Johnny rolled his eyes.

"Never liked him."

I didn't either, but it wasn't my place to say anything. They weren't my family, and I was closer to Johnny than to Olivia. My main concern was for the two girls; Charlotte was thirteen and was in her teenage years, where her main concern should be school and boys. Yet the look in her eyes reflected someone who was much older and was filled with fear and distress. She'd seen someone kill her mom—or, the very least, had heard it all. And she had to hide not only herself but her little sister as well. She most likely had the need to protect her little sister. Ava was ten and still looked ten; she still had that innocent sparkle in her eyes as she hugged her granny and played with her grandfather's cell-phone. She did not see what had happened to her mother; Charlotte had protected her as best she could.

Nigel placed a calm hand on my shoulder, but the gut punching feeling after he motioned for me to follow him left a bad taste in my mouth. I excused myself and followed him outside.

"What's wrong?" I asked before Nigel could say anything.

"I just received video footages of the night Brent said he was at work, and he was not there. We need to show Stephen this."

"What video? Where did you get it from? Billie?"

"No, from an anonymous email. When I replied to the email address, I got a notification telling me it's incorrect."

"Show me." I followed Nigel toward an empty private room where he unlocked his phone and pressed Play. The screen showed the date and time. Nigel skipped through the entire video, and nobody entered the premises fitting Brent's description. "How did he get the alibi then?"

"Maybe the same person who helped him kill her."

I returned to the room to excuse myself and told Johnny we would be back soon. This wasn't something we could tell Stephen over the phone, and, if Brent was at the station, he could answer questions regarding the validity of the video. I recalled Brent's statement where he had given Stephen information and had specifically mentioned a coworker's name with the time he was at work. They had a meeting with overseas clients and had to do a videoconference call.

We arrived at the precinct and asked for Stephen then sat in the same two seat we had the last time we were here. The old man who wore socks with flipflops the last time I'd seen him exited the back area where officers interviewed victims. He wore flipflops again but with different color socks—one white, one brown. He wore board shorts and a dress shirt; it was a very confusing outfit.

"Yes, Carl, we will investigate your claim, and I still have your number," the friendly officer said as he ushered Carl from the office and into the waiting area. The officer glanced over his shoulder at his colleague behind the desk who shrugged in response.

From what I could see, nobody was helping him get rid of Carl.

"Now remember, you do not have to come in tomorrow. Do you understand?"

Carl nodded.

"Good. I'll see what I can do and will give you a call. Okay?"

"Okay," Carl responded but didn't move. He wasn't leaving any time soon.

"Do you need help getting back to the center?"

Carl glanced at the busy street then at the officer. "No. I can manage."

"Good." The officer gently pushed Carl out and closed the door. When Carl was safely out of sight, the officer went to his colleague. "Please stop sending Carl to us. It's a waste of our time, man. I have other more important work I need to get through."

"He's old. He probably doesn't have long to live either. Just be kind."

"His brother has been dead for years, yet he keeps coming in, asking us to investigate his disappearance. He keeps telling us he isn't dead but hiding somewhere, but he can't remember where it is. Carl forgets he's even seen us and keeps coming back again and again. Please don't send him in—if not for your sanity, then for mine."

"Maybe call the nursing home where he lives and ask that they keep him in doors. One day, he might get hit by a car."

I felt sorry for Carl, no wonder he looked a bit disheveled.

"Dana?" Stephen brought me out of my eavesdropping, and we followed him to his office.

Chapter Twenty-Seven

BRENT SCOWLED AT Stephen from across the table. He rubbed his thumb against the bottle of water as he pulled off its wrapper. "I don't like being accused of something I didn't do, Stephen." He exhaled and shook his head. "I didn't kill my wife. And I don't care what that video shows, I was at the office. Lewis was at the office. You can ask him. Bring him in here, you'll see. I don't know why the camera didn't capture us entering or leaving, but we were there." He removed the wrapper completely, rolled it up and stuffed it inside the empty bottle.

"We've already asked Lewis to stop by, and my colleague is questioning him."

"Good."

"Can you explain these websites you are a member of?" Stephen lifted his device, showing screenshots of Brent's profiles.

"Where did you get those?" Beads of sweat formed on his forehead.

"Explain." The screenshots had come with the video

Nigel had received. Someone had sent it anonymously, and not even Billie could follow the trail.

Brent slumped into the chairback, crumpled the water bottle and left it on the table as he glared at Stephen. "I didn't kill Olivia."

"Why do you have profiles on five dating sites, each under a different name that's not your own? Did Olivia know? Is that why you fought with her? Is that why you—"

"I. Did. Not. Kill. Her," he said through gritted teeth. His jaw muscles flexed, and I heard teeth grinding. "I'm not perfect, but I don't hurt women. I'm on a few dating sites, so what? I never met any of them. I just liked to talk with them online, jerk off to their pictures and I'm happy."

"Are you having an affair? Whether you met them on one of the sites or at a bar? Were you seeing anyone else besides Olivia?"

Brent chewed his bottom lip. The silence in the room was palpable. He looked uncomfortable as he squirmed in the chair. "I was having an affair, yes, but I broke it off."

"When was this, and who is the woman?"

"Do I have to? We aren't even together anymore. She had nothing to do with it."

"Let us worry about that, Brent. I want a name."

Brent had given Stephen five names of women he'd had an affair with the last year, all out of state. Two he saw at the same time, while the others one after the other. He had only started looking when Olivia stopped sleeping with him. She probably suspected he had a roving eye long before he admitted it to himself and gave in to his urges.

We sat with Stephen while he investigated the women Brent had slept with. They all confirmed they had engaged in relations with him, but they were all in different states. None of them could've been here to kill Olivia and make it back to their home in time. None of them had traveled recently, therefore we removed them from the suspect list.

As the weight of failure fell upon us, a lanky officer burst through the doors, holding a folder. He almost tripped over his boat-sized shoes as he handed it to Stephen. "Clive asked me to give this to you immediately."

"Thanks." Stephen opened the folder and reviewed the contents.

"Yoh, what's up?" Justin asked. When he saw us sitting there, he arched an eyebrow. "What are they doing here?" He scratched his goatee and sat across from Stephen.

"They're helping out. We have more information here." He handed the folder to his partner then turned to us. "Clive ran the evidence he collected from both Olivia and our skeleton. The cigarette we found near her body contained a chemical compound attributed to lip-gloss. It's the cheap stuff anyone can buy, but the brand of cigarettes was menthol."

Since smoking had been banned in public spaces in 2008, I hardly saw anyone smoking these days, which made it harder to find smokers, never mind which brand of cigarettes they smoked.

"The skin found under Olivia's fingernails has similar characteristic DNA that belongs to Brent, but he'd already said they fought, and she scratched him. Clive did find a partial fingerprint on the shell casing that he is running, and we should know soon who it belongs to. And we found no traces of any kind on our skeleton."

"Could you get ahold of all the women?" Justin asked as he leafed through the folder.

"Yeah, they checked out and are all out of state. There's no way any of them did it."

Chapter Twenty-Eight

TRAVIS

HE SAW her exit the police station with that other PI close by, like he was stuck to her hip. Her cellphone was untraceable, and he suspected she used it under someone else's name—a family member perhaps—but there was no way he could know which, because the variables were just too great. It was difficult for him to find her, and the PI she worked with was a hard man to search, which frustrated Travis. Travis knew Nigel was a *ghost* after he investigated everyone at the agency; they had wiped his credentials clean and provided him with new ones. He knew he had to be careful of that one. Marc was easily traceable and had been a marine for ten years before settling down to be a cop and married.

When Travis discovered it was Johnny's sister who had been murdered, he read the police reports and did some of his own digging. He didn't care, but it was Dana he was helping. A woman had been killed in cold blood, leaving behind two little girls; they would grow up without a mother, leaving them more vulnerable to predators. Travis wouldn't forgive himself if he knew he could do something to help and didn't. The girls were there when their mother had been killed and may have seen what had happened. If the killer ever found out the girls might have seen them, the killer might go after them as well. From what Travis could see, their father was part of it somehow, and he needed to find out how exactly. And, as part of what he and the Horsemen did, they helped those who couldn't help themselves. They assisted the innocent and got rid of the bad, the evil, and the corrupt.

Travis had discovered video footage of the company where Brent said he held his videoconference meeting and couldn't see him entering or leaving the building. He had to share it with Dana, and the only way to do that was by using the agency's email, which he got off the card Aika had received when Dana had visited his company. Then he deleted the account he used to send it from. He didn't know to whom the email would go to, but he had to reach them somehow. He included screen grabs of Brent's wild ways as proof that he was a dog.

Travis watched Dana—the small steps she took when she was calm as opposed to her quick and wide steps when she's in a hurry. Her brown hair was neatly tied and out of her face. *Her face.* He lovingly stared at her. He knew every inch of her body. He'd touched her face and carved his mark. Her skin was paler now, and dark circles had formed around her eyes. *Don't worry, my love. I'll sort this out for you.* She climbed into the blue truck Nigel drove, but that wasn't the person he wanted … yet. He switched on the screen and watched the dot blink orange and move as Nigel reversed out of the parking spot and drove down the street. When the truck turned right, the dot moved right. At least the tracker was working.

The person he wanted stood on the steps and stretched his lean body while he surveyed his surroundings. He shook hands with a tall, dark man as they spoke and smiled like they were at a ball game before he jumped two steps onto the sidewalk. He climbed into the black Audi and drove off.

Travis slowly backed out of his parking and followed the Audi at a safe distance.

Thirty-two-year-old Brent owned a communications company and had dealings with international companies in Beijing and Paris. His work partner, Lewis, was the man with the connections, while Brent charmed them out of their money. Lewis was as dark as night and just as mysterious. He had been called into the police station for questioning from the looks of it; the two men had their story straight as they smiled at each other before exiting and going in opposite directions.

It left Travis white-knuckling his steering wheel. It was up to him to prove Brent's guilt.

Chapter Twenty-Nine

A LOW GUTTURAL sound came from James that I hadn't heard before. With my knuckles, I pushed up his back and massaged his shoulder blade but gently over the scar where the bullet had exited.

"Oh gods, that feels good." He moaned again as goose-flesh covered his back.

Nigel had walked me to my suite to find James fast asleep on the couch with the television on in the background. The case he and my brother were working on seemed to be taking a toll on him, as he'd never come home early for a nap. I slowly crept up to him, and, as I was about to reach for him, he opened his eyes and smiled lazily.

"You're here early," I said, but it was more of a question.

"Yeah. We were at a scene nearby. I think it's the driving that's getting to me."

I sat beside him on the couch when he reached for me and pulled me into the curve of his body. "We're kind of stumped. I was thinking of telling Johnny I'll be heading back. I miss my house and yours. There isn't anything we can do on our side, and they're still waiting for the results from the evidence they collected at the crime scenes. And the skeleton they found points to you know who." I didn't want to say his name while James held me; it would leave an awful taste in my mouth, and I'd have to wash it out with wine. I touched my cheek and felt the faint lines of the scar.

"Good. I think what you need now is your own bed with me in it." I felt him smile into my back.

"Yeah, that's exactly what I need."

"How about we go over there, and I give you that massage you keep asking me for?" He pointed to the perfectly made bed in the next room.

But, instead of him pampering me, we ended up with me giving him a back massage because his shoulder was killing him again.

"Take an anti-inflammatory or something, but you can't continue like this."

"I'll pick some up tomorrow. When's your appointment with Dr. Adams, or did you miss it?"

"No, it's on Friday. That's the other reason why I want to get back home; I've got things to do and appointments to see. Marc says I have new cases I need to start, and he can't keep pushing out the dates."

"If Johnny needs you again, you can come back, but only for a few hours though. You can't stay here indefinitely."

"I know." I kissed the cheek visible and stopped massaging. "Shower?"

Chapter Thirty

TRAVIS

TRAVIS WATCHED the Audi park in a dark driveway, and Brent climbed out, traversed the path toward the front door and entered. Travis parked across the street and killed the engine and headlights. His tablet light was set on dim so his car didn't glow in the dark and alert nosy neighbors to his whereabouts. The report filed by Detective Stephen Fletcher indicated that Brent had mistresses, and the women he mentioned had all been out of state at the time of the murder. Before he could continue reading, his cellphone vibrated in his pocket.

"What's up?"

"Travis, where are you, man?" Joe asked with concerned emotions mixed with his words.

Travis had heard that tone from him countless times and was getting bored with it. He glanced at the date on the screen and realized he was late for a get together. He was so busy trying to get to Dana that he'd forgotten. Even though they no longer needed the support group he had coordinated, they still met at the health center on Wednesdays and his bar on Thursdays to discuss other more important things.

"I'm busy. Send my apologies to the others," he said, not hiding his irritation.

Joe snorted into the phone, and Travis could imagine him nervously running his hand through his black hair. "We need your decision on the latest one." They never discussed names over the phone, ever. Anybody could be listening, even though Travis ensured they all had safe lines.

"Yeah, I know. Tell the guys we need to meet this week-end." They knew what that meant—a get-together at the compound.

"Sure, man. Is there anything else you need?"

"Tell Aika thanks, and I'll give her an update soon." She would know what he meant by that and switched off his phone.

The blip he had been watching while speaking had stopped at a luxurious hotel, and he knew Dana would be staying the evening. Travis made online arrangements to spend the evening there too before switching off his devices and packing them away. He knew enough about the asshole across the road, and he needed him to tell the truth.

The neighborhood was dark enough that Travis didn't need to crouch or walk in the shadows. He crossed the street and Brent's front yard and walked around the back. One light was on in the bedroom, and, as he passed the bath-room window, he heard the shower running.

Once he'd opened he back door—an easy lock to pick—Travis crept through the kitchen, looking for something he could use. He grabbed the large knife from the block and opened the drawers. The bottom drawer had what he was looking for, and he retrieved it. A cabinet was open, and he removed an item from there as well.

Water stopped flowing, and a door opened. Travis froze then slowly peered around the corner. Brent's bedroom door was closed, and Travis headed in that direction. Travis's sneakers were soft against the tiled floor. He stopped near the door and listened to movement on the other side then a light switch clicking on followed by voices —it sounded like an infomercial.

Travis opened a door and switched on the light. Pink bedding flooded his vision as he evaluated the ten-year-old girl's bedroom. Soft teddies sat on her bed, waiting for her return, and a neat desk packed with books and textbooks was against the wall. Her closet was tidy, and she took pride in her appearance. He thought of memories he would've had if his baby sister had lived, and a deep sinking feeling tugged at his core.

The older girl's bedroom screamed teenager, with posters of boys splashed on one side of the wall and a mirror on the other littered with pictures of her friends. Her table looked like a book bomb had just gone off, with papers and files strewn everywhere. Her closet was messy with more black clothing than anything else.

The voices stopped, and a bed creaked. Brent was probably getting ready to sleep.

Travis slowly opened the bedroom door. His eyes had adjusted to the darkness, and he saw the large lump in bed.

Brent must have been exhausted because he didn't stir when the door sounded.

Travis slipped inside the room and quickly closed the door.

Brent turned over.

Travis froze in the dark corner near the door and the side of the closet.

Brent's breathing steadied, and Travis neared. Brent was about Travis's height but nowhere near as bulky or strong.

Travis lifted a piece of the tape he had prepared and stuck on his shirt. He carefully removed it and slapped it over Brent's mouth and sat on him.

Brent tried to sit upright, but the weight of Travis was overwhelming, and Brent's eyes widened in shock.

"*Shh* ... If you want to live, I suggest you shut up and listen." Travis pressed the tape on Brent's mouth then tied one wrist to the headboard with rope he had retrieved from the cabinet.

Brent was too shocked to do anything but stare up at Travis.

"Now lie still, or someone's getting hurt." Travis tapped Brent's chest with the sharp knife.

Brent stilled but kept shocked eyes turned on him.

Travis taped his other wrist to the headboard, as he could only find one piece of rope. He switched on the bedside lamp and leaned with his weight on Brent's stomach. "I know there is something you aren't telling the police, because your wife would never have had enemies bad enough to do what they did to her. If she's anything like her brother, she's practically an angel. It's you who's the devil."

Brent thrashed around, trying to get out from under Travis's body, with mumbling sounds straining against the tape over his mouth.

Travis slapped him so hard his hand stung, but he stilled with moisture gathering in his eyes. "Don't make me repeat myself."

Brent relaxed and nodded, a tear escaping down one side of his face.

"Nod yes or no. Do you understand?"

Brent nodded.

"Good. Did you kill your wife?"

Brent violently shook his head.

"Okay, okay, calm down. Were you at the office at the time of her death?"

Nothing—no movement whatsoever; he didn't say no, so it's a half truth.

"Did you see her on Devil Mountain?"

Brent's blue eyes glistened in the silver light that snuck in from the outside.

Travis sat back and applied pressure to Brent's diaphragm who groaned in agony. "Answer me, Brent. Were you on Devil Mountain?"

Brent mumbled his response, frantically trying to get out of his restraints, but the weight from Travis's body was greater.

Travis slapped him again, harder this time, and the left side of his face turned a darker shade of pink. "Do you have something to say?"

Brent nodded violently.

"If I remove this and you yell, do you see this?" Travis lifted the knife from the kitchen and pressed it against Brent's cheek until a red dot formed.

Brent nodded, wide eyed.

"Good. Now remember, if you yell, I will use it on you." Travis roughly ripped the tape off Brent's face, making him wince.

Brent sucked in air, and Travis sat upright, not liking the feel of Brent's body pressing up against him, and he wondered if Brent was enjoying it more than he was afraid.

"I did lie to the police about only seeing them at the ice cream parlor." He swallowed hard. "I wasn't happy with how we left things. I followed them to their campsite, and, when the girls were in the tent, I called Olivia over. I needed to speak to her. And I left her alive. I didn't kill her."

"What were you fighting about?"

A strange calm settled over his body as Brent resigned himself to what had happened. "She found out about the other women. A friend of hers saw one of my profiles on a dating site and cornered me about it. When I denied it, she said she was taking the girls camping to think about our relationship and that I too should think about whether I wanted to stay or not. It made me realize what an asshole I'd been, and I begged her to forgive me. I broke ties with all the women I'd been seeing." Using his shoulder, he wiped away a tear. "I'd only been seeing one woman at the time, and I didn't give her name to the cops."

"Why not?"

He sighed, and his nostrils flared. "She's well known to the area, and I didn't want the cops to home in on her. It would've been unnecessary."

"Who is she?"

"She didn't do it, man."

"What's her name?"

Chapter Thirty-One

CHARLOTTE AND AVA were in the process of being discharged, but Stephen was there to question them before they left. Brent had shown his face but was asked to remain in the room where he could see the girls, but they couldn't see him. Charlotte was adamant that she didn't want to see her father. I felt sorry for the girls; they needed their dad, especially during such a traumatic event, but, if Charlotte was upset with her dad, I didn't blame her for her request. She needed time to heal.

"Can you go over the events of that night one last time, please?" Stephen asked carefully. It was only Charlotte in the room with him, as Ava was still not talking to anyone else besides her sister and grandparents.

Charlotte looked out the window while she reminisced. "Mom and Dad were fighting during lunch. They sat at another table while Ava and I watched them from our booth. Mom was crying while Dad spoke in low, hushed tones. I don't know what they were talking about, but it made me sad to see Mom like that. And Dad looked angry.

Then Dad left, and we went to the campsite. On our hike, we spotted two wooden carvings. You know the ones?"

Stephen nodded.

"Those doll heads freak out Ava, but I counted thirty on our trail. And it was nice that it was just us girls, and we had the entire camp area for ourselves. Ava and I fetched wood while Mom prepared dinner, then we ate. We counted stars as they started to shine in the sky, and we went to bed. Mom left the tent to use the bathroom, but she was gone for a really long time. When I looked out the tent, I saw her speaking to a person wearing a dark hooded top. Mom saw me and turned that person around so they couldn't see us. Mom's expression scared me, and I didn't know what was happening. But, when I saw the gun in their hand, I knew we had to get to safety. I woke Ava and told her to put on her shoes, and we snuck out of the tent and hid. The person was furious and fought with Mom. It sounded like a woman and looked like a woman, but I don't know."

Charlotte's expression remained the same—filled with sadness yet trying desperately hard to be tough; I'd seen that expression many times to know the difference. To me, it looked like Charlotte had taken over the role of their mother for Ava's sake, and it would be large shoes she needed to fill.

"I told Ava to look away, to stay hidden, but I watched the person lift their hand and aim the gun at Mom. I looked away then. I was too scared to watch. It sounded like a scuffle, followed by silence. Then, after a short while, the gun went off. It was so loud, but I covered Ava's ears in time. That's when I lifted my head and saw Mom lying in a ditch, and there was nobody else. But I was worried the person was still around, looking for us, and I was afraid they wanted to hurt us too. I grabbed Ava's hand and dragged her down the mountain." She choked on her words as her chin trembled.

"Thank you, Charlotte. I know this is very difficult for you," Stephen said as he lifted the piece of paper. "The composite sketch looks great." He pointed at the pencil drawing the sketch artist had made based on Charlotte's descriptions, but unfortunately, the picture looked like a lot of women. Unless we had more detail, like an eye or hair color, it would be almost impossible to see who it was. "If you see this, does anything else come to mind?"

She shook her head. "No, sorry."

"That's fine." He stood and placed the paper inside a folder. "I understand you'll be staying with your grandparents for a while. If you remember anything at all, you can phone me any time." He handed her his business card.

"I want to see my daughters," Brent said when Stephen entered the little room we were in.

"Give them time, Brent. Allow them to heal, and when they are ready, then go visit them. I'm not a psychologist, but your kids need to heal." Stephen placed a calm hand on Brent's shoulder, and he sat down again. "Do you have anything further to add? Remember anything else? Anyone else?"

"No." Brent shook his head.

"Now what?" I asked.

Stephen was quiet for a moment, contemplating his next words. I didn't think they could do anything else. They were still waiting for some results, but, unless it produced something substantial, there were no other leads. "Justin and I will be reviewing the case again and have brought in another detective to assist."

Brent cleared his throat and stood. "I have work to do."

One side of his face had been turned away from me,

but, when he stood and the light caught it, and I had to ask, "What happened to your face?" I pointed to the bruise near his eye; it was faint, but I could see it.

"I hit my head on the doorframe, Sherlock. And mind your own business," he said and left.

"What's his beef with you?" Stephen asked as we exited the room.

"I have no idea. Since the first day I met him, he's acted like a jerk."

"Hey, Dana!" someone yelled behind us.

We turned to see Johnny wheeling down the corridor with his nurse beside him. She must have called out, because Johnny could never have sounded that girly.

"You're leaving us today?" he asked when he reached us.

"Yes. I have cases waiting for me at work, and Stephen has my number. If he needs our help on anything, he'll let me know. Are you going back home with the girls?"

Johnny had moved to Tampa, Florida so he could be near his recently retired parents in case he needed help.

"Yes. Stephen has allowed the girls to come back with us. We've notified the authorities there that should Brent arrive without prior knowledge, we can call them in."

"Do you think that's necessary?"

"Who knows? Until we have an idea of what really happened, we aren't taking any chances."

Charlotte and Ava entered the hallway with their grandparents close by. Ava clung to her grandpa for dear life as they passed, and Charlotte walked ahead with her arm through her grandma's.

Johnny's nurse pushed his wheelchair, and they left.

Chapter Thirty-Two

MARC WAS SPEAKING with someone on the phone when we arrived at the office. Nigel went to his desk, and I went to the kitchen at the back to make a fresh pot of coffee. The machine was empty, with not a single dirty dish in the sink. Marc most likely didn't want to make any coffee if it was only him and doubted he could drink five cups a day with his ulcer anyway.

Once I had a cup of coffee in my hands, I approached my desk with care. Marc had left three cases for me. The requestors had asked for me personally, and, from what Marc had said, they were anxious for me to start on their cases.

The first case was a straightforward background check; one of our regulars wanted more information on a man she was dating. This was the third check she'd wanted me to do in three months. I worried about her. The constant snooping on her date's history—who they were, who they dated, and what they did for a living—was not healthy for her soul. And, as of late, her relationships didn't last.

The second was for an insurance company I'd helped a few times before. They wanted me to check whether one of their clients was still bedbound, since they had received word she was doing a Coyote Ugly at one of the bars. I sighed. I hated these types of cases. From my experience, it was usually a single mother trying to make ends meet even though she should not be working. Come hell or high water, she could be in pain, yet she would find work just to ensure she could feed her children, get them to school and avoid having them taken away. Life was not fair for most, and, when they got lemons, they made lemonade—or had it with tequila. But rules were rules; they couldn't claim for benefits if they could work.

The third case had an envelope inside with *Look: Two for One* scribbled on the front. It left a prickling sensation on my scalp, and my breath caught in my throat.

"Where did you get this, Marc?" I asked, panic evident in my tone.

"Why, what's wrong?" He stood and came around to my desk.

Nigel had heard, and he too approached.

"It was slipped under the door. One for you, and one for Nigel. I didn't want to open them in case they were private, but the look on your face tells me otherwise."

"It was a massacre," Nigel said from behind me, and my arms pebbled again.

"What was in your envelope?"

"Nothing of importance," Nigel said. "Definitely not what you have."

We stared at the scene I held in my hands. It was a handful of color pictures with people gunned down at a restaurant. In the corner at the back were three bodies—a woman, man, and a boy—possibly a family of three. All three had been shot near the same table. The boy lay slumped over the table and faced away from the camera, the woman was sprawled on the floor with two bullet wounds in her back, and the man had a bullet in the back of his head as he seemed to have tried to cover the woman in vain.

Behind the counter on the floor lay a man with a name badge that read MANAGER. Bullet wounds peppered his face, obliterating it. There was no way they could have identified him. I suspected they had to use his fingerprints or dental records. Another male laid face down with his hand outstretched and still held the package he had purchased. His blood had mixed with the package, making it look like a strawberry milkshake surrounded him.

In one frame, in the far corner, was another family—a woman and her two sons with bullet wounds to their heads. At first glance, I wanted to say execution style, but it could also be that the shooter had a semi-automatic weapon. Blood splashed on the floor and walls like someone had thrown red paint, trying to make art.

"What does this mean?" Marc asked as he took the pictures from my hands.

"I don't know." I pushed out my chair, the grating sound like fingers down a chalkboard, and stood. I made a beeline for the door and yanked it open. The bell chimed, and I slammed it shut. I sucked in deep breaths once outside. My chest rose and fell as I tried to steady my breathing, but it wasn't working. Dark spots filled my vision, and a headache blossomed behind my eyes. I placed my hands on my knees when I doubled over and stared at the concrete.

"You okay?"

I flinched at his voice. "Jesus, I didn't hear the doorbell."

"Sorry," Marc offered and joined me outside. "When last did you have a session?"

"I have one this afternoon."

"Good."

Without looking at Marc, I could see him nod out the corner of my eye.

"You can't carry on like this, Dana. It's affecting your work. I hate to say this, but you either need to find something new or take time off and heal."

I knew he was right. Crime scenes were starting to freak me out more and more. I could hardly look at photos, and it was affecting my job. If I wanted to continue doing this, I had to get my head straight. I nodded my agreement.

"There was a number on the back of one of the photos. Nigel will look into it for us. You, on the other and, sort yourself out. I don't want you broken."

I stood straighter and pushed my body against the wall. The cool, hard surface beneath me was comforting. My lungs didn't burn, and the stars I'd seen earlier had evaporated, and I could see shapes clearer.

"What time is your appointment?"

I glanced at my cellphone. "In a couple hours."

"I suggest you read a book and avoid working for the rest of the day. But ..." He exhaled audibly. "I know you. You'll just do what you want in any case."

I smiled; he knew me too well.

Chapter Thirty-Three

I'D SEEN a handful of psychologists over the four years but never connected with any of them. I'd first met Dr. Adams in the hospital after Pig-head carved his signature into my cheek. Dr. Adams had left his business card and said I should contact him if I wanted to continue my therapy or if I just wanted to talk. He even offered a discount to those victims who had succumbed to violent attacks. That put me squarely into that box, although I hated being referred to as a victim.

The bland two-story building sat downtown, with its naked trees, few parking spaces, and quiet hallways. There were other doctor offices, but by the time I would arrive for my appointments, most of them had already seen their patients and were going home.

As I entered the building, a chill caught me off guard, a stark contrast to Dr. Adams's warm office. His receptionist wasn't in, and his office door was open.

"Hello?" I called first before peering around the door-jamb, ensuring he was in there.

"Come in." He sat at his oak desk, and behind him was a shelf filled with the *Diagnostic and Statistical Manual of Mental Disorders* library. The other shelves featured a mixture of nonfiction on true crime. Near the door and large window was a couch for his patients and a chair where he sat. I closed the door, went straight to the comfortable couch and plonked down with an audible sigh.

"Talk to me, Dana. What's been happening?"

Focusing on the trees outside, I rambled on about Olivia's death, her girls, and what they endured. I also told him about the nightmares. When I fell silent, I heard him move from his desk to sit across from me. "Then today, I kinda had a mini panic attack when I saw photos of a crime scene."

He nodded. With his elbows on the armrests, he steepled his two index fingers and pressed them to his lips. "Have you been doing your homework?"

I sucked in my bottom lip and bit on it. The pain immediately shot up my face, and my cheeks tingled.

"Dana, you know the therapy I provide is based on how you gain the control you've lost, to take charge of your fear and distress by changing the way you think about your experience. What you went through was awful. I wouldn't want anyone to experience it. And the fact your line of work may put you in contact with more perpetrators of a similar caliber is frightening. You need to overcome what's keeping you down. You must write down your fears, write down your experience so you can take hold of your emotions and move forward."

I stared at the coffee table between us and the magazines on top. "I did start, but I never finished."

"Do you want to get well?"

"Yes ..." I glanced up with my mouth parted in a surprised *O*.

"Then act like it."

The lump in my throat doubled in size, and I choked on my tears, swallowing them uneasily, and the back of my throat ached.

"Some believe my therapy may come across as harsh, but, if my patients aren't invested in their wellbeing, how do they expect me to be?" He arched an eyebrow. "There's a pen and paper over there. Do it now."

I wiped the tears from my eyes, grabbed the notepad and pencil and jotted down what had happened, along with how it made me feel. I included my fears as well, that I would fall victim to Travis, Pig-head, again and that I might not make it if he ever got hold of me again. I also included that I was fearful for James's life, Travis had warned me before that he didn't like James being in my life. My shoulders slumped as I sat back against the couch and pressed the notepad against my thigh as I wrote. "You do understand that until this guy is captured or killed, there's no real recovery for me. I'll be looking over my shoulder until I meet him face to face."

"And the way you can manage that is by managing your fears and doing what's in your control. It's not you who has the problem, it's him."

I lowered my leg so I could see Dr. Adams.

"Certain things are out of your control, and there's no way for you to control another person's behavior—only your own," he said gently. His words came across as meaningful and caring.

I felt better after my session, and, as much as I hated Dr. Adams's tough love, he was right. I couldn't control what wasn't my fault. And I could only do what was in my grasp. I can't prevent everything from happening.

With that in mind, I wanted to find out what Nigel had learned about that picture. I dialed his number with no response. I dialed Marc next, and he answered.

Chapter Thirty-Four

MY FEET WERE on the coffee table as I flipped through the channels. Nothing seemed interesting enough for me to stop and watch. My laptop made that familiar ping sound, alerting me to a new email. I threw the remote onto the table and picked up my laptop to see Billie had sent us an email.

After my mini episode at the station and while I was at Dr. Adams's office, Nigel had contacted Billie, asking him to find out all he could about the photos we had been sent. After a quick search of the number on the back of one of the photos, he had discovered the case was an old one from the nineties near Devil Mountain. That sinking feeling had enveloped me when Marc had told me. This new case may be linked to our current one, or it related to Eugene and Travis. I had no idea how it related, but one thing I did know, I had to stop thinking about it until I had all the facts. I needed to stop speculating about these cases, as it caused unnecessary stress. It bothered me who had sent it to us, and more importantly, why were they helping us and not the police directly? If someone knew something that had happened to Olivia, they should've gone to the police. But somehow, I knew who it was, and, for the life of me, I couldn't understand why he was helping us.

Similarly, with Eugene's report, this case wasn't recaptured onto the new system, but instead, it was left in a box in the basement. The only part of the case they had captured was the case number—not even the victims' names. Nigel had then contacted Stephen who would assist us in retrieving the report, and Nigel was on his way back from fetching copies, which he'd already sent to Billie to decipher. All this was happening while I was at home, waiting impatiently for Billie's input—until now.

James allowed the front door to slam as he entered the lounge, holding our dinner. "Why did you order so much?" he asked as he wrestled the food onto the table without any of the containers falling.

"I didn't know what I wanted to eat, and everything looked so good on the menu, so I picked a few items."

"This is more than a few." He handed me the box donned with an illegible scribble, but I could make out the words *Chow Mein*. I had a soft spot for Chinese food.

With a mouthful, I opened the attachment with information on the photographs I'd received of the family of three—the woman, man, and a boy—who were shot at one of the tables. The owner had said they frequented once a week. The manager with the bullet wounds to the face had left behind two children. He had been a stellar worker, and the owner couldn't give enough praise. The man who was lying face down with his hand outstretched and still holding onto the package was there to collect food for the family and had stepped into the massacre. If only he had arrived ten minutes earlier or ten minutes later, he would've lived. I guessed the same could be said for all of them. Next was the woman and her two sons; it was their first time, as they'd just moved to the neighborhood. Billie had no other info on them, and the identity found in the woman's purse was illegible. The only way they'd known they were new to the area was because nobody recognized them and by the newly signed lease agreement found in her purse for a nearby apartment. But she hadn't included her full name or social security number, as she had paid in cash.

The shooter had stolen cash from the register and from the deceased. They left fingerprints at the scene, but there were no hits. This happened in 1990, and the database was just getting started. Stephen indicated he would be running them again to see whether anything came up on CODIS.

As I read the owner's name, I dropped my fork into the food container. "It's the same ice cream parlor Nigel and I were at. It's owned by Sally and her daughter now." I scanned the email and read it had been her dad's shop when the massacre had happened. "Someone is trying to tell us something. We need to speak to Sally and find out whether she knows or remembers Eugene, Travis, or Olivia."

"Not now you aren't." James pointed his fork at me. "Finish eating, get some rest then you can go hunt her down tomorrow."

Sulking, I grabbed my fork and had another mouthful while I continued reading the email.

Chapter Thirty-Five

I WATCHED Annabelle open the doors to their ice cream parlor and lock them behind her. Sally wasn't with her, but it wouldn't hurt asking Annabelle in the interim. I climbed from my car, walked across the street and knocked on the glass door.

Annabelle startled, obviously not expecting anyone so early.

I waved, plastering a smile on my face so I didn't scare her further.

"Hi. Sorry, I can't remember your name. You were here asking about the Greens?" Annabelle surveyed the area, ensuring I was alone.

"My name is Dana. I was wondering if your mom was around or on her way here?"

"Why?" she asked suspiciously, her brows knitted together.

"Or maybe you can help me. I read there was a shooting at your ice cream parlor years ago where people were killed—"

"Ooh, you want to know about that?"

I nodded.

"Well, come on in. Mom's busy with a delivery and should be here shortly. Lock the door when you come in please." Annabelle flicked the switch, and the shop came to life. The metal counter was spotless and held a sparkle to it once the light was on. "Hope you don't mind if I work while we talk. Mom prefers everything to be ready by the time she gets in."

"No problem, if you don't mind sharing what you know about that day while you work."

"Mom was sixteen when it happened. She and Grandpa were supposed to be at the shop that day, but he had car trouble. It's weird how things work out, but—"

A knock on the door caused us to turn to see who it was, and Sally waved back at us. Annabelle opened the door for her mom, and I felt awkward sitting while the owner of the shop entered.

"Dana, this is the second time you are speaking to my daughter. Should I be worried about something?" Sally's tone and smile didn't match, and I knew I had to tread carefully to avoid upsetting her.

"I was actually looking for you."

"True, Mom. She just got here and asked me one question."

"What question?" Sally demanded, her tone softer but still sharp.

"As I was saying to Annabelle"—I pointed to her—"a case was given to me, and I wanted to find out a little more about it."

"Involving us?" Sally asked, taken aback.

"Yes, the shooting that happened here in 1990."

"Oh, why would you get that case? It happened so long ago."

"That's what I need to find out. Sorry, I know it's strange, me coming here and asking these questions, but I'm trying figure out if or how the shooting here relates to one of our current cases. It's all very cryptic, I know, but, if I don't follow all leads, I'm not doing my job."

Something caught Sally's eye, and she turned toward the window.

I followed her line of sight and only saw the back of someone walking away.

"What do you want to know?"

"Did you see any of it happen?"

"I don't remember much. I was sixteen. My dad's car broke down, so we couldn't go into the shop, and he asked his manager to open for him. He was a great man, Mr. Fryday, had two kids. Their mother had died from cancer the year before, then their dad was killed—sad really. I think they went to stay with relatives. The others were just patrons and were killed for their money. They never did catch the killer."

Going through the shooting victims might not be what was required. *Look: Two for One* was written on the envelope with the photos. I still wasn't sure what that meant. *Two for one* could mean two things for the price of one, or two things happened here, but so far, we only knew of the one. Or perhaps I had to *look* at the parlor. I spied the tables neatly in a row with four chairs per table. The walls were a soft white that didn't hurt the eyes when the lights were on. The counter was new and made from glass so the desserts were visible inside, beckoning the customer to take one home after they've eaten. In the back was the kitchen, and in the corner was the soft serve ice cream machine and beside that were the different flavor ice cream tubs to select from. Nothing seemed strange about the place. Perhaps I needed to *look* at Sally, *look* at Annabelle. I didn't know what it meant. Annabelle looked sweet and cuddly in her milkmaid outfit with her ridiculous puffy sleeves and milky-white dress and blue apron. Her brown hair was neat and tied back in a ponytail. Her big blue eyes stared innocently at me. Annabelle was the complete opposite to her mother; she was full of smiles with a bubbly personality, while her mom seemed tightly wound the more I got to know her. Sally wore a loose-fitting navy skirt and white blouse, and her grey hair was also tied in a ponytail. The only jewelry she wore was a gold necklace with a locket decorated with fine engravings.

Perhaps I was wrong about this, and there was no connection, but then why were we given the photos? No, something had to be here. Annabelle said she didn't know Eugene, but perhaps Sally did. That could be the connection, the *two for one*.

"Another question that may or may not be related to the shooting. Annabelle has already spoken with us, but perhaps you might now. Did you know Eugene Lawrence?"

Sally opened the counter door, retrieved napkins and folded them into triangles. "No, can't say that I do. I don't recall the last name Lawrence as one of the victims." She considered then shook her head. "No, I'm sorry."

"He wasn't one of the victims, but he was murdered."

"Oh goodness, no. Sorry, but I don't remember him."

"Travis Green perhaps?" It felt like I was grasping at straws, and they were made from razorblades.

"I knew of his parents, and I'd seen him around, growing up. He was younger than me, so we didn't really mix in the same circles. They were only here for certain times of the year, if I remember correctly."

The next thing I had to know was whether she knew Olivia or Brent and had she seen either of them the day she had left with the girls to go camping. Charlotte had said they ate a late breakfast before their hike and that they had waffles. Stephan had already confirmed they were here after he spoke with Annabelle.

"Last question then I will leave you to it. The woman who was first thought missing then ended up dead, Olivia is her name."

Sally nodded.

"Do you remember seeing her with her two daughters? I understand they had waffles here before going on their camping trip. Or her husband, Brent?"

"I wasn't here that day. I was busy with deliveries. Did you see them, Annabelle?"

Annabelle nodded her head. "I already spoke with Detective Fletcher."

"Thank you for your time."

Chapter Thirty-Six

TRAVIS

TRAVIS WATCHED her exit the ice cream parlor, cross the street to her car and climb in. He turned the key, and his Mercedes purred to life.

She reversed out of her parking spot and drove away, him following close behind. She stopped at a house, and just when Travis thought she would pass by, she turned quickly, almost knocking over the mailbox. It was such a sudden movement, he didn't think she would make the turn. She sat in her car for a while, not doing much, from what Travis could see.

He drove past, circled the block and parked a few houses down but could still see her car.

She climbed out her car and entered the house without knocking.

———

TRAVIS WALKED around the side of the house and headed for the back door, hearing raised voices. He crouched and listened to them yelling at each other near the window he was underneath. She was shrieking, telling him it was lies and that he should mind his own business.

Travis knew what they were arguing about, so now was the time to confront them. He opened the back door and found Brent wide eyed, his fists gripping Annabelle's shoulders, trying to get her off him, and her hands were around his neck.

"Who the hell are you?" Annabelle asked, anger and frustration laced in her words.

"Let go of him." Travis raised the weapon. "My, oh my, for someone who's soft and gentle to the outside world, you're quite dangerous behind closed doors." Using the gun, he pointed to where they had to go.

Annabelle released Brent's neck, neatened her shirt and walked ahead of them.

Brent coughed and rubbed his throat.

Travis closed the back door and followed them into the lounge. "Sit."

Annabelle sat on her own while Brent sat on the couch farthest from her.

Travis pointed the gun at Brent. "You lied to me, Brent."

"What's he talking about? Do you know this creep?"

"I would shut up if I were you, darling," Travis said.

Annabelle closed her mouth into a tight line.

"Speak," Travis said to Brent, who had slumped into the couch.

"I didn't lie to you." He panned from Annabelle to Travis. "I was seeing both of them."

"Mother/daughter team, I get it, man. I really do, but you lied to me. Do you know what I do to liars?"

Brent shook his head as beads of sweat peppered his forehead.

"Sometimes I remove a foot, a finger, any appendage they won't miss."

Brent swallowed hard. Travis watched his Adams apple bob up and down.

"But your kids have already lost one parent. I won't hurt them. But you need to fix that."

"I know. That's why I've broken it off with both of them. I wanted to come back home. I wanted Olivia."

Annabelle shot Brent the dirtiest look Travis had ever seen.

Brent ignored her. "I wanted to work it out with Olivia. I was in the process of making amends. I was a foolish prick—"

"Jackass ..." Annabelle said, crossing her arms.

"I broke it off with Sally and Annabelle on the same day."

"Right. That's why I'm here." Travis stepped closer to Annabelle and pressed the pistol against her head. "Did you hurt Olivia?"

Annabelle shook her head so violently Travis recoiled; otherwise, he'd have hit her on the head. "I swear, I would never. I read she died of a gunshot wound. I don't even know how to use one. And neither does my mom."

"Who was driving your mom's car that night?"

"I was."

"I retrieved the trips the car took during the day from the installed tracker, and it stopped at Devil Mountain around the time of Olivia's death—"

"It wasn't me, I swear. I stopped by Brent's place, and he told me we were over, and I went home. I drank some of Mom's wine and fell sleep."

"You're telling me it's your mom?"

Annabelle shrugged.

No cameras were in the area except those at a traffic light a few miles away. The tracker had logged the trip, and the car had been in the parking area near the ranger's cabin where it had stayed for three hours—enough time to avoid the ranger, run to the campsite, kill Olivia and run back.

"Why are you doing this? We are nothing to you, yet you're trying to solve this case. Dana is involved, and the cops are working on it. Who are you, and why do you care?" Brent asked, the lines between his brows deepened.

Travis pondered it a second time and couldn't devise an answer he wanted to share. He'd been watching Dana for four years and had gotten to know her really well. She'd been suffering since their initial encounter, and he couldn't help but think it was all his fault. Witnessing his parents' murder and growing up without them had left a stain on him. He had avenged their deaths and that of the sister he'd never met, but he still felt empty. The hurt and cracked void in his chest didn't go away and didn't fill up. The emptiness stayed, and he felt hollow. His time with the others in the support group had taught him a lot; nobody wanted to be harmed or left alone. Those who had hurt others—innocents—were no worse than the criminal who had killed his parents, the evil doers who hurt his friends. Yet, it was in him to hurt those who hurt others—a vigilante at best. He was a protector of innocents.

Yet … he was the one hurting her.

As much as he didn't want to get caught, he felt bad for harming her. He was confused; he had never felt this way. *Ever*. She had changed him. She had made him a new man. That was why he was helping her. He wanted to see her happy, to see her smile again. The last few times he'd seen her, she'd lost her spark. She was having nightmares, unable to do her job to the best of her ability, all because of him. He had to make it right, had to help her. And this was how he knew he could help her, by nudging the culprit her way.

"Just think of me as a guardian angel," Travis said and smiled sinisterly.

Chapter Thirty-Seven

"IT WAS a waste of my time, Marc. I swear, I don't know what the hell is going on, and everything is just confusing me."

"Why don't you come home?"

"I want to go to the crime scene one more time. Stephen said it was okay and instructed one of his officers to escort me there. Perhaps I can spot something now that cops aren't swarming the place."

The officer nodded when he saw me climb from my car to head to the ranger's cabin.

"Okay, has Nigel checked in with you yet?"

"No, he was supposed to give me copies of the report last night, but he never showed. I assumed he went home and would call me today. I guess I forgot to see if he was in the office."

"Let me know if you find anything while I try to get hold of him."

We ended the call as I reached the ranger cabin.

"Ma'am," Officer Spencer said with a curt nod. He

wore his uniform but had swapped his patrol shoes for hiking boots. "The ranger gave us the go-ahead." He pointed at the trail and waited for me to pass him.

"Please call me Dana, Officer Spencer," I said and walked ahead of him. "I don't suppose you could give me an update on this crime scene?"

"No. I'm not actively involved in the case. Today is actually my day off."

I stopped and turned around. "I'm sorry, and you decided to put on your uniform?"

"Yes. Stephen said I should so you could recognize me."

"Oh, well, thank you for being here. I appreciate it, and especially on your day off." I turned and continued walking.

The trail was scenic; tall trees surrounded us at first, but the higher we traversed, the greener it became with more green bushes and rocks. Again, I spotted doll heads tied to branches high on trees and purposefully avoided looking at them.

We reached the campsite within the ninety minutes they said it would take. The yellow tape was still there, but the markers were long gone. Forensics had taken Olivia's tent for processing, and, in its place, more tape and flattened grass.

I went to the area where her body had been discovered. At first, I walked around the tape while Officer Spencer stood to one side, giving me space. I lifted the tape tied around a tree to enter. It hadn't rained since Olivia's death, but fine dew drops covered the grass, making her visible blood beneath the wetness shine a deep red. I crouched to get a better look of the flattened blades of grass, the large bloody area from Olivia's head wound, and the disturbed sandy area where someone most likely stood and moved on the same spot without leaving a print.

The team had most likely collected everything they could find in this area. I stood and ducked under the tape and branched out a bit. Taking a wider girth, I circled trees that grew closely together until I was on the other side and crouched again. I glanced at the trees, the grass, the disturbed area. I wasn't searching for anything in particular but doing this—*looking*—sometimes helped me put things into perspective. I could stare off and think of the case and maybe, just maybe, something would come to me.

As I started to stand up, to my left, something caught my eye. I focused on the spot without looking away so I didn't lose it and approached. The sun had caught the object at such an angle that it reflected light.

I grabbed a stick to dig the object from its hiding spot in the sand and lifted it up. "Officer Spencer! You might want to look at this!"

Heavy footsteps neared, and Officer Spencer pulled an evidence bag from his back pocket.

I arched an eyebrow at his efficiency.

"Detective Fletcher said you seemed to find things and I should come prepared."

I smiled. "I will be sure to thank him for the confidence." I allowed the object to fall inside the bag, and he closed it. "I've seen someone wear something similar." I pulled my cellphone from my pocket.

Sally wore a gold necklace with a locket that had fine engravings etched into it; this necklace looked strikingly similar. I phoned Stephen and told him what I'd found and that the envelope with photos weren't just coincidental; someone had already known the women were involved. That Annabelle, who seemed so sweet and meek, might have killed Olivia if this was her locket—or the very least knew who did. One thing for sure, Annabelle had been here. I circumnavigated the campsite but, other than the necklace, couldn't see anything else.

As I traversed a different trail, Officer Spencer ran after me. "Where are you going now?" he asked breathlessly.

"I want to visit the other crime scene."

The wide hole was left undisturbed after they'd removed the skeletal remains. Yellow tape surrounded the foliage and wrapped around trees and a peg, making an off-rectangle shape. The fallen tree had been moved to the outskirts of the tape, and insects continued crawling in and out of their holes. Inside the hole, protruding roots made it a proper grave. The dry leaves had been swept away and left in a pile to one side, and, farther up, more holes were dug.

"Do you know what they were looking for up there? There's at least ten holes here."

Officer Spencer's brows knitted together, and I didn't think he'd been here before, so he might not be able to answer my question. Instead of answering me, he scanned the multiple holes, grabbed his radio and called it in. The serious way he did it sent a shiver up my spine.

I glanced at the holes and back at him. He was asking for back up. The first thing that came to mind was it wasn't the cops. Someone was here, looking for something, and all I could think of—it was Travis.

I flinched when birds flew through branches and squawked.

Twigs snapped, and Officer Spencer drew his weapon and pointed it at something behind me.

Turning slowly, I carefully surveyed the area but saw nothing out there. The wind blustered, branches swayed, and leaves rustled. It could've been an animal that had scared the birds. Shaking off the sensation of being watched and thinking nothing else could be found, I returned to the trail and lowered Officer Spencer's arm. "I don't think anything's out there, Officer. I think we can head back now."

He holstered his pistol and followed me down the trail. I felt eyes on me through the entire trip to the ranger cabin. It might have been the doll heads in the trees or the wooden carvings of men I'd seen or even Officer Spencer, but I couldn't help but think it was Travis, Pig-head, lurking in the shadows of the mountain and watching me.

Chapter Thirty-Eight

OFFICER SPENCER FOLLOWED me to the police station where Stephen had already summoned Annabelle and Sally. As we entered, I overhead the desk sergeant comment about Carl, the one who wore socks with his flipflops and mismatching outfits. "I'm worried. He's never missed a day coming here, and we hadn't seen him for two days."

"But you told him not to come in."

"I always say that, and he still comes in."

"Maybe he fell ill. Perhaps call the nursing home."

I wanted to know more, but Officer Spencer held the door open for me to enter. We sat in the observation room and watched the women sit across from Stephen.

He informed them why he had asked them to come in as well as the case he was working. He gave them Olivia's name, and neither women showed any signs they knew her.

In the other room sat Brent with Stephen's partner, Justin. Brent rubbed his eyes, fidgeted with his watch then continued to twitch in his seat. When I'd first seen Brent at the start of the investigation, he seemed confident and a little smug. Now he looked like someone who was coming off a high and needing another score. His hair hadn't been brushed, his clothing was wrinkled and untucked, and his face was a little gaunt. Something was eating at him. Guilt perhaps ...

"Where were you the night Olivia was murdered?" Stephen asked the women.

"At home," they said in unison.

"Can anyone else verify that?"

"No," Sally said.

Annabelle shook her head.

"We have records here that your car"—he pointed at Sally with the folder in his hand—"was parked at Devil Mountain at the time of her murder. Can you explain this please?" Stephen had received the vehicles trip tracker for that evening from an anonymous source.

"It was her." Annabelle pointed at her mother. "She was out."

"Annabelle? What are you talking about? It wasn't me." Sally shook her head, wide eyes pleading with Stephen. "I went to bed early, like I do every night. I took one of my sleeping tablets and slept. There's no way I was there," Sally said with panic laced in her tone. Then something clicked, and her expression changed to anger. "You were seeing him too, weren't you? I wondered why you were so angry. That was the day he said he didn't want to see me anymore. He said the same thing to you, didn't he? And *you* killed his wife?" Her voice raised, and her expression changed again to the likeness of dread.

It made me wonder whether she thought her daughter could've done something so evil to another woman, and all for a man.

"Brent, please can you tell us who you spoke with on the

night your wife, Olivia, was murdered?" Justin asked on the other screen.

Brent broke down. He covered his face as tears streamed, and he shook his head. He admitted he had been seeing both the mother and the daughter, and, when Olivia had threatened to leave him, he wanted to try again. He wanted to make it work with his wife. That's when he had broken it off with the two women on the same day. He didn't say anything before because they were a well-known family, and it could destroy their business.

Annabelle glowered at her mom, and her mouth pressed into a straight line. "How could you think that? I'm your child ..."

"That I know nothing about. He is so much older than you, Annabelle. Why?"

"I could ask you the same thing, *mother*."

"Did you take my car, honey?"

"No, I swear. Whatever you have there is false. We didn't do it."

"The tracking company confirmed your car was there." Stephen placed the folder on the table and walked to the door. When he opened it, an officer handed him a brown bag, whispered in his ear and closed the door after him. Stephen's actions were slow and meticulous. He peered inside the bag, his face revealing nothing, and sat down again.

Both women fidgeted in their seats. Sally rubbed her hands, and Annabelle gave Stephen a deadpan glare.

"That's a pretty locket you have there, Sally." Stephen pointed at her neck.

"Thank you. I had them made especially for Annabelle and me." Sally glanced at Annabelle. "Where's yours, honey?"

"I lost it," she answered in a monotone filled with hate.

Stephen removed a plastic sleeve with a chain and locket like the one Sally wore.

Annabelle's expression tightened at the realization that Stephen had her chain.

"Does this belong to you?" he asked sternly.

"How did you get it?" Sally reached out for it.

"It's evidence. You can get it back once we're done processing it." Stephen laid it out on the table for both to see. "Annabelle, can you remember where you dropped it?"

"No. It could've been anywhere, really. I could've dropped it at the shop."

"We didn't find it at the shop. It was wedged in mud near the area where we found Olivia's body on Devil Mountain."

Annabelle blanched. Her lips had even paled; she licked them and swallowed. "It was an accident. When she lunged at me, I hit her on the head and ran," she whispered, and the room fell silent; even the room we were in was eerily quiet.

My heartbeat was loud in my ears, and I wasn't the one being questioned. I had nothing to be nervous about, yet I was filled with dread.

Annabelle swallowed again. "All I wanted to do was scare her." Annabelle turned to her mom and mouthed, *I'm sorry*. "I wanted to scare her into leaving her husband."

"What were you thinking?"

"I wasn't. I just wanted to know who this woman was who had Brent wrapped around her finger."

"Really? Is that what you're going with? I can't believe this. He was married, Annabelle! You were the other woman, not the other way around. Heavens, even I was the other woman."

"Please continue," Stephen interrupted Sally chastising Annabelle. "Did you discharge the weapon?"

"No, don't say another word. She needs a lawyer present," Sally blurted, raising her hand to stop Annabelle from replying. "Don't say anything else, Annabelle."

"No, Mom, it really was an accident. I have nothing to hide. They were at the shop, having an early lunch, and I overheard Olivia say they were going camping on Devil Mountain. After you fell asleep, I took your gun and went there to confront her. All I did was wave it around, and she lunged at me. I hit her on the head, dropped the gun and ran. She must've grabbed my locket when she went for me." Annabelle pulled down her shirt to reveal a faint scratch mark on her chest. "I saw this when I got home. At the time, I didn't think I'd lost my locket. All I thought about was being arrested for assault. But I swear I didn't kill her."

Chapter Thirty-Nine

"ONE OF THEM IS LYING," Stephen said as he repeatedly clicked his pen.

"We still don't know whether Brent was actually at work when he said he was at work, and his witness isn't exactly reliable. He's changed his story twice since we last spoke with him, which puts Brent front and center," Justin said as he entered behind Stephen, holding a steaming cup of coffee.

"But Annabelle just admitted to being there. She could've killed Olivia," I said as I stood.

"And it's been days, so we can't test her hands for gunshot residue," Stephen said.

I paced the room's limited space. "Olivia scratches Brent the same time they fight, and Annabelle witnesses this. Charlotte saw a woman in a black hoody, so, even if she said she saw someone with Annabelle's description, it doesn't matter, because she's already said she was there. Now all we have to do is determine which of them actually pulled the trigger."

"We need to find the gun." Stephen turned to Justin. "See if we can search Brent's home."

Justin nodded.

"If Annabelle parked out front, where would Brent park? Are there other spaces where someone can park and enter the hiking trails without the ranger noticing?"

Stephen and Justin stared at me like I had sprouted a third eye.

"What?"

"There is another way inside. I used to go that way when we were kids," Stephen said, while Justin agreed. "And I don't think anyone bothered to check it out while we were out there."

"We kinda had our hands full," Justin said dryly. "We've had enough to keep us busy for a few months."

"Yeah, I think we should check it out now then swing by Brent's house," Stephen said. To the officer who had arrived with them, he added, "Keep them in their rooms until we return."

———

FOR NOW, they couldn't charge either of them, but I suspected it looked like they were both guilty. I followed Stephen and Justin's cruiser to Devil Mountain, but instead of going straight to the parking area next to the ranger cabin, we turned right onto a slip road. We drove for a distance, and when I thought we were going nowhere, they stopped on the right-hand side of the sand road. I parked beside them and climbed out.

An old fence surrounded the large area, and where we parked was a gaping hole big enough for a small car to drive through. Near the hole were tread marks and footprints. In one section, it looked like drag marks.

"Didn't you say someone brings those large carvings and places them in areas for hikers to find? What if he uses this as his entry point?" I asked as I walked on the grass; I didn't want to disturb any treads or footprints.

"We thought the same thing," Justin said. "On our way here, I spoke to the ranger about this person, and she says she's never seen him. He left her a note about five years ago, saying this is what he's done. He only wanted to showcase his carvings and to make the hike adventurous for young kids and adults. He didn't want the owners to get upset and remove them. After that note, they just let him be and allowed him to do it. The ranger also said she suspected he found another way in, because she'd never seen anyone dragging a big-ass wooden man around." Justin slipped through the hole with Stephen following.

I entered behind them and followed the path marked with days-old footprints. We traversed the trail, pushing thick tree branches out of our way. The vegetation was thicker, the path unclear, but I followed the men. We climbed between rocks when there wasn't anywhere else to go, and, when the men stopped, I couldn't see why. Their large backs blocked my path, forcing me to walk between them, and I stopped.

In the middle of our path was a campsite for one. His *tent* was comprised of old tree stumps and branches, and a tarp covered everything. There was even a chair carved from a rotting stump. Whistling sounded in the distance, and, before we could hide to not spook the squatter, he came around a rock and swallowed his whistle, but his lips stayed puckered.

"I don't mean no harm," he said, dropping the wood in his arms and raising his hands.

"It's okay," Stephen said calmly. "What's your name?"

"Kevin."

"Kevin, my name is Detective Fletcher. That's Detective Fleming, and this is Dana Mulder. Would you mind if we asked you a few questions? You aren't in any trouble or anything like that."

Kevin nodded. "Can I lower my hands?"

Stephen nodded. "How long have you lived here like this?"

"A good few years. Mind you, I don't know what year it is." He chuckled. "I do like the quiet here, and I don't bother nobody."

"Are you the one making holes to trap animals?" Stephen asked.

His eyes widened. "Yes, sir. I have to eat. I only catch once a week. That's it, I swear."

"It's all right. One of our men fell inside one of your traps, and we were wondering who could've done it. And now the case is solved," Stephen said with a smile. "I don't suppose you've seen anything strange? Or anyone come by this side besides us?"

Kevin averted his eyes. "Maybe. In all the time I've lived here, I hadn't seen nobody else use this side. But a few nights ago, one fellow came by and then another one. That's two different men on two different nights. They didn't see me. I'm good at camouflaging. And now today, I see you three." He pointed at us.

Stephen showed the man something on his cellphone.

"Yep, that's the one."

"He just ID'd Brent," Stephen said, returning his phone to his pocket.

"He came through that way." Kevin pointed at an area below that looked easier to walk through. "Then a couple hours later, he's running down the mountain like the devil was chasing him. He had blood all over his face, and he was crying. It scared the bejesus out of me. It's not often I see someone covered in so much blood, you know."

"How did you know it was blood and not mud?"

"Blood shines red when the moon is bright." He headed toward where he said the man had walked. "Here." He pointed at a tree. "He gripped this tree so hard 'cause he almost fell, and there's more blood." Kevin pointed to another tree with smears.

Stephen pushed through to look.

Justin was on his phone, calling for the tech team.

Stephen took photos, and I came around the other side to see blotches of smeared blood where the *man* had gripped the young tree.

"This looks like a fingerprint." I pointed to the side where I stood.

Stephen followed my line of sight and snapped a few shots as well.

"The team is on their way," Justin said as he pocketed his cellphone.

"Kevin, do you remember where this man had come from?"

"Like I say, he was running like a bat out of hell from that direction. If you continue straight and take a left, you hit the campsite." Kevin continued walking. "Now, that other fellow, he was smart. He walked carefully, like he'd been here before, like he knew the area well. He kept looking around to make sure he was alone, as if he sensed I was nearby. It made me feel uneasy, especially after I saw that first fellow with all the blood. But I followed him to make sure he wasn't going to hurt nobody, and he went to one of the sites with that yellow tape. Then he did the strangest thing. He started digging. He was looking for something. After about an hour, he found the box, most likely put it there himself and then just forgot where he had buried it. Anyway, he packed the box in a bag and left. He didn't walk the same way he came though. That's how I knew he'd been here before, because he took another route I sometimes take that leads me back to my entrance." Kevin pointed at the gaping hole in the fence.

"Can you tell me what he looked like?" I swallowed the lump in my throat and wiped damp hands on my jeans. If this was Travis, I needed to know what he looked like. It felt as though I was driving blind on a highway onto oncoming traffic. I could pass this man and not know it was *him*. It would be dangerous for me to continue and not know his appearance.

"He was as tall as this fellow." He pointed at Stephen who was about six feet tall. "Brown or dark brown hair, light eyes. They could've been blue or green, I'm not sure. He was pleasant looking, if you know what I mean. Could drive any girl crazy if he wanted to." He wiggled his eyebrows.

This did not help. He had just described any good-looking guy. "Thanks, Kevin. Do you remember anything else?"

"He drove a nice car with one letter on the number-plate." Kevin glanced up, pulling his face. "It was a big S."

That awful sinking feeling I would feel whenever I thought of Pig-head before I had known his name was Travis returned, and I touched the butt of my gun—a reflex. At least I wasn't hyperventilating as I thought I would have, thanks to Dr. Adams's treatment and cognitive behavioral treatment. *I'm in control of my emotions. I could do this. Nobody is chasing me ... yet.*

He was here. Travis was here because he knew I was looking into him. But something was here he'd buried with Eugene that he needed, something he would risk being discovered. Something very important, perhaps evidence or something from his past he didn't want anyone to know, especially now. To the business world, he was an important man, but, at night in the shadows, he was something else. He was a vigilante killer, and he preyed on others. He was a predator and hunted me. I was only doing my job; what he was doing was illegal and morally wrong. It was not only that he had killed people, but the way he did it—violently and bordering on torture.

I flinched when my cellphone rang, fished it from my pocket—which I almost dropped—then answered.

"Nigel is missing," Marc said.

"How do you know?"

"The signal for his cellphone is dead. He would never do that. He knows I would be looking for him."

"Have you checked the hospitals—"

"He's nowhere to be found. Billie sent his picture to all the hospitals from Devil Mountain all the way past Chicago, and he is nowhere. The police haven't picked up anyone who looks like him either. He's gone. Something happened to him."

I didn't want to say this out loud, but Travis was in the area and knew we were looking into him. It was possible he'd seen Nigel working with me. All those times I'd felt as though I was being watched, maybe I had been. And I knew Travis was the one helping us with Olivia's case by sending us the videos and pictures. Why? Was it possible Travis wanted to get me alone, or did he have another motive for going after Nigel? Did Nigel do something in his past that crossed with Travis? Surely Nigel and Marc would've said something before if that were true. No—there had to be something else.

"Dana? Are you still there?" Marc asked.

I ignored him and ended the call. I didn't know why, but I knew I had to go to the ice cream parlor. There had to be another reason why we were sent those pictures; it couldn't have been a coincidence that it was only so I could question Sally and Annabelle about Olivia's death. There had to be something about the massacre itself.

Look: Two for One. I said the words over and over. *One*, I had to investigate Sally and Annabelle and their connection to Olivia. *Two*, I had to consider the people who had died in the massacre—the family of three, the manager, the man who was picking up food, and the mother and her two boys.

My blood ran cold as I remembered what Nigel had said: his wife and two boys were killed long ago.

As I passed Stephen, I told him where I was going and why. He said he was coming with and called backup.

Chapter Forty

TEN SQUAD CARS with flashing blue and red lights surrounded the ice cream parlor. A man with a megaphone called out to the person inside to exit with raised hands.

Someone in the center of the parlor had their hands up, but they were unmoving.

The same man with the megaphone said something to someone beside him grabbed his binoculars, swore and told everyone to get inside, along with a paramedic.

My heart dropped to my shoes; someone was hurt.

The police rushed inside, but Stephen told me to stay outside and watch through the window.

What I saw made me physically ill. I retched near a trashcan, wiped my mouth on my sleeve and went back.

Red covered the once-white parlor—the walls, tile floor, and counter. The edges of the maroon puddle on the floor were darker as it dried, while the middle was redder where blood still dripped from the body. He was suspended by his wrists, bound to either side of the wall. His chest was bare, with engravings etched into his skin: *Mass Murderer*.

I was aghast as I took this in. I felt helpless even though I knew I had to do something; what that was, I didn't know. I watched uniformed officers leave markers and take photos, with Stephen pointing at objects he wanted photographed.

One flipflop had fallen to the floor, while the other one dangled from his foot; a blue sock covered that foot while a black sock covered the other. He wore three-quarter pants that hadn't been washed in a few days, and his floral Hawaiian shirt was on the floor, drenched in his own blood.

The Frozen Sundae, 1990

THE HUTCHINS FAMILY entered The Frozen Sundae for the first time since moving to the area. They placed their orders and sat.

Wayne quickly licked ice cream from his fingers as another drop ran down his cone, licking that one too. It was a messy affair. But a deal was a deal; if Wayne and Lewis finished all their chores, Caroline would treat them to an ice cream. It was a way for her to spoil her boys and to make up for them missing their dad.

"Quickly, Wayne, before you mess on your new pants." Caroline scooped another spoon of strawberry-flavored ice cream into her mouth.

Lewis burst out laughing as he watched his brother lick his hand. Lewis was smart; he chose a bowl, like their Dad preferred when he was around. He wasn't fond of cones because they always made a mess. And today was hot, and the shop was hot; no amount of air conditioner would keep the ice cream from melting and making the cone soft and gooey.

Wayne licked his hand then chomped on his ice cream. He too could eat ice cream without any pain, just like his dad. Except, he preferred to enjoy his ice cream slowly, but today, it was melting too quickly. As he took the last bite of his dessert, two things happened at once: an ear-piecing noise made his ears ring, and warm liquid splattered his face. He dropped his cone, pushed his chair backward, bent over to allow the stuff to drip off his face and blindly reached for a napkin on the table to wipe his face, all the while wondering where the thick liquid had come from.

Shouting erupted around him. Another blast sounded, and more liquid sprayed his left side. Chairs scraped across the floor. Wayne heard his mother whimper beside him, but it sounded like bubbles instead of words. His brother yelled then went eerily quiet.

Mr. Fryday, the manager they had just met, pleaded with someone while another customer begged. There was another blast, and something hit a table and dropped to the floor.

Wayne wiped his face and opened his eyes in time for the bullet to hit.

———

CARL SEARCHED each of the wallets and purses and removed all the money from the cash register, making today's hit one of his best. He made an easy five hundred. He ran from the parlor, where his brother was waiting for him in their getaway car.

"Hurry," Kevin said as he revved the engine.

"I'm coming." Carl climbed in.

Kevin mashed the gas pedal, and they sped off before the cops neared.

"You didn't have to kill them, Carl," Kevin said in a moan beside him.

"Do you want to score or not?"

"Not like this, brother, not like this. You promised me we wouldn't hurt anyone." Kevin took a left corner and headed for Devil Mountain. Kevin white-knuckled the steering wheel. "I can't keep doing this, Carl. After the last one, you promised me we wouldn't hurt anyone no more. You promised—"

"I know, but they saw my face. I couldn't have that. They describe me to the cops, and they will come for you too."

"I'm done." Kevin stopped the car. "Get out! Get out, or I'm taking you to the police station myself! I'll turn you in so fast your head will spin."

Carl opened the door and slowly climbed out. "You're making a mistake, brother. A big mistake."

"I don't care. You and I are no longer brothers. Do you hear me? You are sick, Carl, sick!" Kevin sped away, leaving Carl on the side of the road with money in his pocket but nowhere to go.

Chapter Forty-One

BRENT BLINKED AT STEPHEN, not answering the question.

Stephen leaned back into his chair and repeated the question. "Did you see Annabelle assault Olivia, and then, when she left, you grabbed the gun she had dropped and shot your wife?"

A knock on the door made Brent flinch in his seat.

Stephen opened the door, and an officer handed him a piece of paper.

Brent stared at it deadpan.

So much was happening simultaneously. Stephen was questioning Brent following the discussion with Kevin while his partner, Justin, was at the ice cream parlor murder scene. They'd processed Carl's fingerprints and got a positive match to the 1990 massacre. I asked for the victims' names and learned the mother and her two sons' last name was Hutchins—Nigel's surname. His family had been gunned down on the same day of their arrival into town. When I had first received the photos of the massacre, Nigel also received an envelope, and I suspected inside was the answer to his family's murder. He didn't tell us about it, because he wanted to sort it out himself, and now he was missing. It twisted my stomach into knots that Nigel had lost his family and had become like the vigilante killer we were hunting ourselves. Now that he was missing, he was wanted in connection for Carl's murder.

I'd questioned the officer who always tended to Carl about the brother he kept saying was missing. The officer had told me his brother's name was Kevin. I informed him about the Kevin at Devil Mountain, and he had someone fetch him to identify Carl's body. As it turned out, they were brothers, and the local department arrested Kevin for his part in the massacre. He had peacefully offered his wrists for handcuffs with a satisfactory smile, welcoming his punishment. Kevin was in his late fifties and would most likely die in jail once the trial concludes.

CID processed Annabelle and charged her for assault with a deadly weapon. Sally got her a lawyer who was helping her through the procedure. The state prosecution would ask for no less than five years, serve two.

Brent hadn't said a word nor had he asked for a lawyer to be present.

Stephen pushed a piece of paper in front of Brent and tapped it with his index finger. "You left a partial fingerprint on the tree when you ran down the mountain and on the gun we found at your house. The rifling of the bullet from Olivia's body matches the radial pattern of the gun in your possession." Stephen placed another piece of paper in front of him, showing the gun they had found after they had searched his house during his arrest. "We also have an eyewitness who puts you at the scene that evening." Stephen pushed another piece of paper in front of him with a picture of the cigarette. "We know you smoke this brand. At first, it was strange, because we found traces of lip-gloss, a similar shade Annabelle wears, but you smoked after you had kissed her. She was there that night, or she saw you. That's what set off Olivia. She saw the two of you after you had promised your wife you wanted her, which makes me believe the two of you planned this from the beginning. Unfortunately for you, any money you thought was coming to you is going to your daughters. Olivia amended her will a year ago already."

Brent's expression changed as his mouth tightened into a straight line.

"And your partner, Lewis, sang like a canary after we threatened to charge him with obstruction of justice. He told us your meeting was cut short that morning and not the evening. It's another charge we have against you. Talk to me, Brent. I can't promise you a lesser sentence, but I can tell them you were cooperative."

Brent sat back, lifted his hands above his head and stretched. "She didn't want to divorce me, you know. She said if I was desperate for one, she would make sure I left with nothing. She wanted to make me grovel for monthly maintenance. She even threatened to take my company from under me. I couldn't have that." A malicious smile crept up his face. "I gave it another year, but I couldn't anymore. And, as much as I love my girls, I hated Olivia more. God, that woman was painful to live with. 'Pick up your socks, put your dishes here, don't leave that there,'" he said in a high-pitched voice, mimicking Olivia. "The worst was when she stopped letting me touch her. I mean, what is a man to do? I got it elsewhere. And yeah, I followed Annabelle there, watched her yell at Olivia." He laughed.

"It was priceless. But when she lost her nerve and dropped the gun, that's when I took charge and took care of it."

The way Brent said it, made my blood boil, like Olivia was trash he had to take out. He didn't have an ounce of remorse or regret, and I hoped he served a very long time behind bars.

"What were you going to do with your girls? They saw what happened."

Brent averted his eyes and shrugged. "Luckily, I couldn't find them," his said nonchalantly, like the mere thought of killing his kids was just some part of his plan.

I shuddered as I watched.

"Afterward, I ran down that mountain so fast I tripped over a root and landed on my hands and knees. As the pain shot through my limbs, I stayed in that position for a few seconds to catch my breath. All I thought about was what I'd done. The cool air burned my lungs as I panted, but all I smelled was Olivia's blood on my face, hands, and clothing. My palms stung as I squeezed the soil and dry leaves." Brent rubbed his fingers together for added effect. "I smelled the debris. The moist soil and leaves took me to a time when I was young and went hunting with my father." His creepy smile had returned. "And, for the first time in years, I felt free. It was one of the best nights of my life. I was free of her whining and free from her perfect life. I was just free." He sat upright and leaned his elbows on the table. "I told Annabelle to shut her mouth, but the stupid kid couldn't."

"You'd never get away with it, Brent. The evidence against you was too great." Stephen rose from his chair and towered over Brent. "And we are pushing for the death penalty."

Brent jumped up to grab Stephen, but Stephen

slammed a fist into Brent so quickly he didn't have time to react and slumped back in his chair.

Chapter Forty-Two

I STRETCHED my limbs and felt beside me.

James was already up and somewhere.

I climbed out of bed and was thankful it was Sunday—lunch at the parents' day. I heard talking and found James in his study on the phone.

When he saw me, he called me over.

I entered his study, walked around his desk and sat on his lap while he spoke.

He wrapped an arm around my waist and pulled me closer. "Right, so it's closed now?" He nodded and watched me with a lazy smile. "Good. Thanks, man. Chat later." James ended the call and placed his cellphone on his desk.

"Everything okay?"

"Perfect, just perfect. We're tying up loose ends on that case, and it should be finished soon. When that happens, I'll tell you all about it." He cupped my face and kissed me. "I made coffee if you want. What should we have for breakfast?" he asked as we entered the kitchen.

"Just some coffee for now. And don't forget we have

lunch with my parents. You know how Ma gets when we aren't hungry."

James chuckled as he poured me a cup of coffee. "Have you heard back from Nigel?"

"No. Marc is still looking, and now Stephen and his partner want him for questioning."

"You know who orchestrated this, don't you?"

I nodded. "Travis. He used his program to find out about Nigel and set him up. He turned Nigel into one of his vigilante killers and then kidnapped him."

"His family was gunned down in cold blood, and he wanted justice. When that was handed to him on a silver platter, he fell for it, unfortunately."

"I know. I get it, I really do. I realized I didn't know Nigel at all, but he looked so … normal."

"Looks can be deceiving, Dana."

"I know. I'm not a child."

"I'm not trying to fight with you."

"Please, can we just stop and start over? I was having such a good morning."

James handed me my cup and pulled me into an embrace. "How about we go to your parents' a little early today? I'm sure your mom would love it, and I'll ask Donnie to do the same."

"You know, that sounds like a wonderful idea. A day with you, my brother, and my parents would be perfect."

"Yeah, especially after the week you had."

I nodded into his chest. "Especially."

Chapter Forty-Three

TRAVIS / MR. GREEN

THE HORSEMEN REGARDED their newcomer with excitement. They had prepped their weapons and were ready for the chase, the hunt, with someone who might be a little difficult to catch and kill. A little challenge never hurt anyone.

Miss Red—otherwise known as Aika—turned to Mr. Green. "Who's turn is it today?"

"Well, as you know, I haven't had a go in quite some time. Would anyone mind if I went today? It would make me very happy to have this one all to myself." Mr. Green glared at Nigel. The scowl he received in response only made his blood boil with excitement, and he couldn't wait to get started.

Nobody objected. Everybody knew that when it was one Horseman's turn to hunt, they had twenty minutes to complete the task. Should they fail, it was open season, and anybody could take the last shot. But, because Nigel was such a fine specimen and came with experience, Travis—

Mr. Green—had put something in his water to make him more compliant.

Nigel climbed to his feet, swayed but held onto the bars to keep him steady.

"I think he is ready," Mr. Green said as he headed for the stairs.

The Horsemen followed and stood back while Mr. Green opened the gate.

"You have a minute, Nigel," Mr. Green explained. "Once your minute is up, know that I am coming for you."

"Then what?" Nigel slurred.

"Well, the game is to see how long you can last. There is no way out of my compound, nobody can hear your screams, and, if you hurt one of us, understand you will suffer the consequences."

"S-s-so it's fine to hurt me, but I can't hurt you?"

"Absolutely not. This is our game and our rules. I'd get running if I were you." Mr. Green started counting backward from sixty.

Nigel exited the cage and staggered out of sight as he went behind the games building.

"Right, let the hunt begin." Mr. Green ran toward the other side of the games building to catch Nigel on the other side, but, as Mr. Green rounded the corner, Nigel was nowhere in sight.

Mr. Green headed for the trees on the far side where Nigel could've hidden. As he maneuvered toward the building, he heard screaming overhead. Mr. Green looked up as Nigel crashed onto him.

Fist after fist connected with Mr. Green's face as Nigel pummeled him.

With the hunting knife Mr. Green had in his right hand,

he thrust up and into Nigel's side as he lifted his arm and twisted the knife inside.

Blood sprayed everywhere, and Nigel buckled.

Wiping blood off his face, Mr. Green felt his nose was broken, but it was nothing compared to what he was about to do.

Nigel crawled on all fours to the building. Before he reached it, Mr. Green rammed his knife into his side and kicked it deeper inside with his foot. Screams pierced the air as Mr. Green grabbed the handle and pulled the sharp blade down and back up.

Intestines spilled onto the grass below Nigel's body, blood sprayed everywhere, and he fell onto his side. Nigel tried to scoop up his intestines, but it was futile; it wouldn't be long now.

"Holy shit!" Mrs. Platinum shrieked beside Mr. Green. "That's gross."

Nigel gargled blood, leaned his head against the wall, and his arms fell limp to his sides. Gravity pulled his body to the ground where he died.

Mr. Yellow—or Joe—pulled Nigel's body into the building where an oven was already prepared at the correct temperature: 1400 to 1800 degrees Fahrenheit.

If there was no body and no witnesses, then there was no crime ... in Mr. Green's eyes.

vinci-books.com/chasingevil

**Travis wants her as his trophy. But now, she's hunting
him.**

Travis's deadly game of cat and mouse will only end with one of
them dead. Dana has had enough. It's time to take back her life
and stop him for good.

Turn the page for a free preview…

Chasing Evil: Chapter One

The hard concrete beneath my bruised body was awful. When I tried to move onto my side, my hips digging into the ground was not pleasant. I gave up on trying to get comfortable and rolled onto my back even though my spine and shoulders ached.

As to what had happened—*he did*. As much as I wanted to forget everything—*I couldn't*. The memories were still fresh in my mind, like a bitter pill I kept choking on.

My tongue stuck to my palate when I swallowed, and I craved an ice-cold glass of water. Slowly I sat up. My surroundings were dark and unknown. There were iron bars for walls, with the night sky for a ceiling. Behind me was a large house at least three stories high made mostly from glass than brick or wood. The second story had a large balcony, and when I rocked onto my tiptoes, I could discern a bar area to the side with the doors wide open. Someone was home and had left me *here*—in a freakin' cage like one would keep a large animal. In front of me was a yard of sorts; I wasn't quite sure what kind of yard, but it was large.

I couldn't tell where the wall began and the trees ended it was so vast. I mostly saw shadows and outlines of trees, with another building in the distance.

My cage contained no luxuries. The floor was concrete with dark spots I could only assume was body fluids from those before me. I imagined the state those poor people had been in when they were brought here, awaiting their ultimate demise—their bodies bruised and their minds broken. It wasn't the law that had brought them here or any medieval knight but six people who lived the vigilante lifestyle, but instead of bringing the guilty to justice, they held their own court where the person was only guilty in *their* eyes. Handing down a death sentence to all by way of a sport; with the wide-open spaces, I imagined the person running for their life with nowhere to go. Only the fastest could survive for long, but the ultimate price was with their life. I supposed the resulting end would be welcomed after spending time with those six.

Shivering, I hugged myself tighter. My teeth chattered when a wind caressed my skin as I looked for a way out of my situation. I flinched at the voice behind me.

"Dana ..." His voice was so deep I could feel it in my bones. He exhaled. "My god, you were hard to catch." Before, he'd always worn a mask, which distorted his voice, but now, I could hear the real him, and I knew who *he* was —I could recognize that voice anywhere.

I turned in his direction and rubbed my arms for warmth. "You!"

Chasing Evil: Chapter Two

Wednesday

I sipped my coffee while my laptop switched on. Marc was in the kitchen, fetching a cup of the delicious black liquid I had made. Nigel was still missing after five days. Marc and I had split up and visited all the various hospitals, police stations, and morgues, showing staff pictures of our colleague, our friend, but he wasn't there. He wasn't injured, arrested, or dead. He was just *gone*—vanished into thin air.

Marc knew of family members Nigel had back West, but they hadn't heard from him since a mass murderer, Carl Bingham, had massacred his family during a robbery in an ice cream parlor near Devil Mountain while his brother Kevin drove the getaway vehicle. The two had escaped capture for over fifteen years until recently.

I had received information on the ice cream parlor and what had happened years ago on the same day Nigel had received an anonymous letter, detailing Carl's name, address, and a recent photo. We had found this letter in his desk drawer while we were busy searching for anything on why or where he had disappeared to. Nigel had driven back to Devil Mountain to fetch the police report for me, but he didn't stay there nor did he come home. Instead, Nigel had sent Billie photos of the report instead of dropping the copied files with me. Then he had gone after Carl himself. Nigel had found Carl and butchered him—tied his wrists and stretched him out in the center of the ice cream parlor, cut up his abdomen and watched him bleed to death. Then Nigel had disappeared.

For five days, we had been searching and still nothing.

I continued with my case load while Marc did the same. Neither of us wanted to say the obvious, to say what we thought—that Travis and his vigilante killers had gotten hold of Nigel. The killers got *rid* of him like they had so many others before him.

It was a vicious circle; revenge killings never ended. Someone would always get hurt—someone left alone once they had lost a loved one. This madness wouldn't end until we stopped it. I wasn't sure how this would be done, but we needed to find Travis and the rest of his group and either kill them ourselves or try turn them over to the police. The problem was they were a hard bunch to find, and we had no idea who the rest were. I suspected Aika, the exotic-looking assistant at Seekster, was one of them. The types of questions she'd asked me and then stared in my direction were obvious clues she was involved in more ways than just as an assistant to Travis, but it was hard to prove.

We needed to get our hands on a few things: proof of who they were, proof of their involvement in any of the murders, and their dealings with Travis, along with signed statements. But there were no bodies, no eyewitnesses, and no proof. I was toying with the idea of gaining Aika's trust and getting information from her, but I had no idea how far she was into Travis's game or if there was a way to bring her in. Johnny and I had spoken extensively about this, and he was trying to do things on his side with the FBI, but nothing had been agreed upon yet, so it was up to us to do *something*.

My laptop chimed continuously as the emails loaded one after the other. None of the emails were about Nigel, so I sat back and finished my cup of coffee first before I answered them.

The doorbell chimed when a delivery guy entered with a package. He scanned the clipboard in one hand and checked the address on the package then stopped before my desk. "Are you Dana?"

"Yep." I stood to receive the package.

"Sign here please." The delivery guy handed me the clipboard.

I did as requested and swapped it for the package.

"Here you go."

Once he had left, I used my scissors to cut one side open.

"What's this?" Marc asked over my shoulder.

"I don't know." I arched an eyebrow. "I can guess who it's from though, and I won't lie, I'm a little afraid to know what's inside."

"Do you want me to do it?" Marc placed his mug on my desk and reached for the scissors in my grasp.

"Sure," I said, handing them over.

Marc cut away the tape, placed the scissors on the table and lifted the lid from inside the packaging. He dug both hands inside and removed a vase. "There's an inscription."

Marc read it to himself first then handed me the vase. "Now we know where Nigel is."

"What?" I asked, understanding what he'd said but not registering. The vase was a midnight marble blue with a silver lid. On the side was an inscription beautifully hand-crafted in calligraphy: *Here lies Nigel, Father, Husband, Friend.* I opened the lid to ensure and saw ashes; whether it was Nigel's was up for debate.

"They really did get to him."

"Of course, they did. They sent him information about his family's deaths, and he did what most would do—he went after the guy responsible for taking them away. They did this to lure him out on his own. Then Travis could catch him for himself and did who knows what to him." I returned the vase into the packaging and grabbed my mug with shaky hands.

"From what we've seen before, it wouldn't have been pretty."

I'd seen the photos of how Travis and his group tortured and maimed their victims, and it wasn't pleasant. Their imagination was scary, with the tools they had at their disposal.

"What are your plans for today?" Marc asked, changing the subject. He obviously didn't want to dwell on our discovery or the pain Nigel must've endured at Travis's hands, and neither did I. But that didn't mean I was about to sweep it under the carpet; we would figure out something and soon.

I placed my mug on the table and clicked on my calendar. "I have a nine o'clock. I'm handing over evidence to my client, then I'm out for the rest of the day."

"Okay, and you're only doing surveillance, Dana," Marc

chastised without me even doing anything wrong. "I don't want any hero stuff." He arched an eyebrow.

"I know, but just so you understand, if I'm attacked first, I will protect myself."

"I know." He averted his eyes and clicked something on his screen. "We are building evidence to take through the proper channels. We can't have you running around like a cowgirl, getting up to no good. And just because Travis isn't after you, at this moment, doesn't mean he isn't watching you."

I understood all too well what was at stake, because it wasn't just about revenge or stopping a bunch of killers; this was about justice and putting all of them behind bars. This was about their victims, no matter how bad they might have thought they were. What they had done was wrong and needed to be brought in—all of them.

My nine o'clock entered. I handed her the photos of her boyfriend, and she was not pleased, as expected. He'd professed his love to her, but he was also a gold digger. He had other girlfriends, other wealthy girlfriends, and once I'd contacted the others to let them know who they were dating, they all dumped him. And my client would be the next one to do the same.

After my client left, I packed my laptop, greeted Marc while he was on the phone and left the office. The drive to Seekster was forty minutes in traffic. Once I arrived, I found a parking spot across the street from the monstrous building and waited. I answered emails on my laptop, and by eleven, I packed it away, sat up straight and fastened my seatbelt. I noticed the raven hair before I saw her face.

Aika exited the secure building, crossed the street and into a parking garage. She didn't park underground of the building she worked in; instead, she parked across the street. It was strategic for her to do so; it was a way for her to come and go undetected. The garage she used did not have any cameras nor did it have a person collecting the money. She paid for her ticket at the machine, climbed into her car and left; nobody saw her come and go—no witnesses to her actions. Except me.

I pulled from my parking spot and followed her bright red Mustang. We drove for about twenty minutes until she pulled into the driveway of a home in Winnetka. This was not her place; she lived in Oak Brook. Every day at this time, she stopped at this same address. I had no idea who lived here, but I would change that today even if I had to jump over a fence to see inside. The last three days, I'd been following Aika to get a feel for her routine and to see where she lived. I now had her home address—which was very different to her driver's license—and I knew what she preferred to eat for dinner. Sometimes the job was boring and mundane, but I had to do this; I had to learn more about this group and try to put a stop to them.

At first, Marc did not want me doing this, to follow her, but she was all we had. We did not have an address for Travis, and we didn't know who the others were. I'd first told Marc about the feeling she had given me when we were at Seekster and the types of questions she had asked and how she had said them to try to convince me she was involved with Travis in more ways than one. Only then did Marc agree that I keep an eye on her but only at a distance, and if I kept my current cases up to date.

I circled the block and stopped around the corner where she couldn't see me nor could the person who lived in that house from their second-floor window.

After two hours, Aika exited and drove past. The last few days I'd tailed her, she went straight back to the office. Today, curiosity was gnawing at me, and I wanted to see for myself who lived in that house.

I climbed from my car and circled the block. Only one row of houses comprised the large block, and the target house sat between two other houses. Instead of going in front of the houses, I came around the back, hoping to see something—anything. The walls of that house were about six feet high and without a back gate. The house on the left had a gate, and the walls were lower; the house on the right didn't have a back gate either. I tested the handle on the gate for the left-side house, and it opened.

I waited to hear barking after the gate had clicked open, but when no attack dog appeared to maul me to death, I knew it was safe for me to enter. The back yard was large, and the house was quiet. The windows were devoid of curtains, and I couldn't see any furniture. From the emptiness of the house, I surmised it was unoccupied. I closed the gate behind me and followed the path to the house. When I reached the porch, I could see into the mysterious yard. A large pool sat behind a house made mostly from large glass panels that reflected light, and I couldn't see in.

As I was about to descend the stairs, movement caught my eye. Someone had closed the sliding door. Perhaps they were leaving. I needed to see who they were and where they were going. For Aika to come here every day must mean this person was important. It could be Travis or one of the others.

I ran down the stairs toward the gate. Once I reached my car, I climbed in and turned the key. A moment later, the black car drove past. I inched forward and saw the target house's gate close. That black car belonged to the owner of the house. I turned right and followed.

Grab your copy...
http://vinci-books.com/chasingevil

About the Author

N. Gray is a USA Today Bestselling Author who lives in Cape Town, South Africa, with her daughter and adopted cat named Miss Beans. During the day, she's an analyst and provider profiler for a medical insurance company. At night, she types on her curved keyboard, creating fictional characters some may love and others you may want to kill yourself.

She writes in four genres: urban fantasy, thriller, horror, and paranormal romance.

She now writes under Natalie Michaels for her new thrillers and SD Syns for her new horrors.

Acknowledgments

Thank you to my dearest best friend, Angelique. You have been my ultimate fan, and I'm lucky to have you by my side.

Also, to my family: without you, I may not have gotten this far.

And to my editor, Brian: he has been awesome, to say the least. I'm sure he laughs at my South African slang, but he always gives me the right American terminology, and I'm grateful for his input.

Lastly, to my readers, thank you for reading!